MW00948732

There is a
Generation II

To:

Aaron Cleaver

W.H. Buzzard

There is a Generation II

KIDS OF THE GREATEST GENERATION

~

W H Buzzard

Copyright © 2015 WH Buzzard
All rights reserved.
Cover photograph of face in water tower copyright © 2015 WH Buzzard
All rights reserved.
There Is a Generation II is a work of fiction. Where real people, events, establish-
ments, organizations, or locales appear, they are used fictitiously. All other ele-
ments of the novel are drawn from the author's imagination. The characters are also
fictitious and are not meant to represent any real, living persons, institutions, or
organizations.

ISBN: 1512180289
ISBN 13: 9781512180282
Library of Congress Control Number: 2015911886
CreateSpace Independent Publishing Platform
North Charleston, South Carolina

Cast of Characters

Timothy ("Tim"): an adventurous young mischief-maker
Hector ("Hect"): orphaned school dropout and Tim's best friend
Tim's mother: married but basically raising Tim as a single mom
Tim's father: alcoholic who spends his time at cushy rehab centers
Ms. Dronaman: friend of Tim's mother and her closest adviser
Rosa: street girl in Juarez, Mexico, who befriends Tim
Raul: Rosa's brother and Tim's guide into the desert
Bernardo: Mexican farmer/pastor who wants Tim to stay in Mexico
Victor: Bernardo's friend and Rosa's uncle (*tio*)
Juweel (Ju): the camp commander originally from South Africa
Centipede: camp recruit leader and psychopathic tyrant
Bum-Eye: Hect's name for the partially blind recruit who helps Tim
Agent # 2: unnamed spy whose nerves are shattered
Acey Elu: a delusional, ambitious genius who created the camps
Man in turban: the lecturer in the films shown at camp
Man in beret: interpreter for the man in the turban
Border guard: a customs agent who interviews Tim and Hect at a border crossing
Spirit: imaginary (supposedly) friend to Acey Elu as a child
Pepe: the name for Tim's hand puppet
Red: red-haired recruit who tries to entertain in place of Tim

Table of Contents

Cast of Characters · v

Introduction · xi

Chapter 1   The Camp ·1

Chapter 2   The First Ms. ·10

Chapter 3   The Adult Discussion ·20

Chapter 4   Back to Juarez ·25

Chapter 5   On the Trail ·39

Chapter 6   Centipede ·45

Chapter 7   Camp Life ·55

Chapter 8   A Hundred Sit-Ups ·60

Chapter 9   The Death Challenge ·67

Chapter 10   The Water Tower ·74

Chapter 11   The Bitter Water Battle ·79

Chapter 12   A New Camp Tyrant ·86

Chapter 13   Across the Border ·98

Chapter 14   Acey Elu ·103

Chapter 15   A Border Guard ·112

Chapter 16   Breaking the Silence ·121

Chapter 17   Murder ·128

Chapter 18   A Spirit Speaks ·137

Chapter 19   A Spirit Dungeon ·149

Chapter 20   Dead Man'th Pokey ·154

Chapter 21   Attack ·160

Chapter 22 A Wing and a Prayer · 167
Chapter 23 On the Way to...? · 173
            Final Note · 181
            Author Biography · 183

To Marshall, whose friendship saved many lives,
mine included,
and whose wise advice made all the difference.
To Joanie, Editor Extraordinaire.
To Nancy, a number one encourager.

*There is a generation that is
pure in its own eyes,
yet is not washed from its
filthiness.*

*There is a generation—oh,
how lofty are their eyes!
And their eyelids are lifted
up.*

Prov. 30:12–13, KJV

Introduction

~⌒~

IN THE 1950S, THE START of the great American culture shift began. The boys and girls who would one day transform society still played cowboys and Indians, war, or hopscotch. Their parents, who spent the final years of the forties celebrating after the gloom of the Great Depression and World War II, had by the middle of the next decade all but partied out, but not so their offspring, those privileged kids of the "Greatest Generation."

At the end of *There Is a Generation*, West Texans Hect and Tim met a black man in the Juarez, Mexico jail named Juweel, or "Ju," who grew up in South Africa somewhere. Ju wouldn't reveal where he'd been born because of a hatred for nationalism, saying he "belonged to whichever country didn't know he was there."

Ju, Hect, and Tim escaped from jail on the back of a giant truck with balloon tires able to drive over a high-voltage, electric fence. Tim might not have gone, except he unintentionally offended a gang leader of cutthroat convicts. While making their getaway, they clung on the back of the truck's cab, balancing on the bed rails while speeding through the night out into the Mexican desert. Tim burned his hand grabbing an exhaust pipe and, barely able to hold on, at the first bump did a somersault through the truck frame. The driver wouldn't stop, and Tim got left behind. The tumble knocked him out cold. He woke up before sunrise surrounded by a vast desert, which as soon as the sun came up, would begin the countdown to an agonizing death. Lost, hurt, thirsty, and with little hope of ever finding civilization, he started walking.

At long last, he happened onto a broken-down windmill. After Tim made some repairs to get the windmill working, the next night three thirsty mules heard water splashing in the trough and stopped by for a drink. Tim befriended them. One in particular, which he dubbed "Half-Ear," allowed Tim on his back, and the three mules carried him to a farm on the edge of a small village outside Juarez. The farm's owners, Bernardo and Maria, took him the rest of the way to the border of Texas.

Safe at home at last, Tim was surprised by a $2000 check in his name from Trustworthy Insurance Company as a reward for saving them paying losses on a dress shop. The owner of the dress shop set fire to the building in an attempt to collect damages, having stored her inventory in an old shack in a deserted auto junk yard. This same abandoned shack Tim and Hect burned down on a lark, and then spotted a blazing human figure in a window, which turned out to be a mannequin. Not knowing that at the time, the boys began their adventures as fugitives from the law in the belief they were murderers. Despite ending up innocent of the "death row" crime and $2000 richer, Tim could hardly celebrate for being guilt ridden over his best friend who was still out in the Mexican desert somewhere at a mysterious place called "the camp."

CHAPTER 1
The Camp

THE SUN BORE DOWN WITH cremating heat out of a vaulted sky. Even the buzzing flies passed by with what sounded like tiny screams. Four long trailers had parked in a semicircle close by a "town of spirits," as Raul had called the ghost town in his so-so English. Empty buildings in various stages of collapse gave the one-intersection town with its dirt roads a haunted look. The tallest structure in town, a water tower, had a death's-head painted on it. Below the skull and crossbones, the Spanish word **Toxico** had been added. Past the water tower stretched a wide, flat desert whose lonely occupants, whirlwinds, waltzed across a sandy dance floor.

Young men stood motionless in evenly spaced lines. Most looked about my age, fifteen or so, and yet at the same time older somehow. No one spoke, nor did any eye stray from straight ahead. I surveyed the rows of sunburned faces searching for Hect, hoping to find him, despite knowing better. Sure enough, no luck. How sad to come all the way across the Mexican desert to finally locate the notorious hidden camp and, more importantly, to rescue my best friend and end up empty-handed.

Moments earlier, the "boys," as the Commander had called them, entered the mess hall in a most un-boy-like manner. Each one dressed alike in T-shirts and khakis, marching stiff as toy soldiers with not a smile among them. They arrived double-file, every pair of eyes to the front as their boot heels pounded the metal floor like the slow boom-boom-boom-boom of a kettledrum. As they approached, I stood in the middle of a room filled with empty tables, the one out-of-uniform newcomer, feeling like a helpless bug being encircled by red ants.

Once past the entrance, the double-line divided. Both ranks peeled off across the front of the building, marched, turned ninety degrees, marched, went down along each wall, and cut a second squared-off turn. The two lines met at the back of the room, stopped, turned sharply, and faced the center, forming a rectangle in which I wound up the focal point.

"Hi-yaah-tu!" a lone high-pitched voice squealed.

The lines along the walls broke apart at what must have been a command and reformed around each table as if everyone knew their place. No one sat. Instead, they snapped their heels in a single click while remaining ramrod straight.

One young man from out of the crowd went to the front, striding importantly. Tall, lanky, and muscular, his body nevertheless appeared out of balance because of an overly small head. From his broad shoulders down, he was powerfully built, but from his shoulders up his head looked a little bigger than a softball. Unlike everyone else in their T-shirts and khakis, he wore a buckskin suit with tassels and knee-length moccasins fringed in strips of leather. The tassels resembled hundreds of tiny legs and had no doubt been the inspiration for his nickname *El Ciempies* or, as Raul translated for me, "The Centipede." One look at his acne-ravaged face, made even fiercer because of all the pockmarks and pimples, and it became obvious why, again according to Raul, no one called him that except behind his back.

Since our arrival late yesterday, Raul had found out a good bit about our leader in talking with others. Although I'd been knocked unconscious the whole time, they'd told him that Centipede actually came from a border town in Mexico; that he went to school in Texas where he'd learned English; that he'd been recruited early on and that, being a fanatic and cruelly ruthless, he'd achieved his present leadership role. They also said he was very sensitive about his looks, especially his odd-sized head, and to never make the mistake of saying "Centipede" in his presence; that one recruit, who spotted a venomous Texas Redhead crawling up a friend's pant leg, cried out the name in formation, and the leader flew into such a rage that he searched the assembly one by one until he found the quaking recruit, who he then challenged on the spot. The fight that followed was not only one-sided and unfair, but gory beyond description.

The gawky leader lifted both arms, pumping his fists while parading back and forth on the podium. "Ahhh-aha-ahaaa!" he yelled at the tops of his lungs, reminding me of Tarzan's jungle cry in the movies. "Ahhh-aha-ahaaa!"

Everyone around the tables stiffened their posture and clicked their heels again. He slammed one fist into his chest, making a *thud.* The room responded, ramming their fists across their own chests, making an answering THUD that echoed off the metal walls. Not wanting to be the odd one out, I imitated the salute, but too late. The room already quieted. The buckskin-outfitted leader's glance fastened on me. My knees quaked. I'd managed to accomplish the one thing I wished to avoid—attract his attention.

Next, Centipede clapped his hands three times quickly, and the whole room sat down as one, except for me. I'd been so worried about making a poor first impression that I failed to react. This drew yet another scornful glare, but I got down as fast as possible.

Centipede clapped his hands twice and everyone produced a notepad and pencil. He then left the platform. The tension in the room eased. Rather than anyone talking, laughing, or roughhousing, they behaved more like serious students preparing for an exam.

Someone shut the blinds, darkening the room, and a projector shot a beam of light onto a screen near the podium. With a sinking heart, I realized a film would begin any minute, possibly a lecture, judging by the studious looks around me, and everyone had come ready to take notes but me, much like in my school days back home. Fortunately, a problem arose with the projector and the blinds had to be lifted. It was a chance for me to get prepared.

The kid next to me not only had a notebook of several blank pages, but an extra pencil as well. I leaned over close. "Beg your pardon," I ducked my head and whispered in case Centipede might be within hearing. "I'm new here, my first day actually. Would you loan paper and a pencil to me? I have nothing to write with."

I could've saved my breath. The fellow even scooted his writing materials farther out of my reach as if I might steal one. I turned to my neighbor to the other side, but he stretched out a tattooed arm, creating a sort of blockade between us. This seemed odd. Never in all my days as a student had I run into two so unwilling to oblige.

Wary of disappointing Centipede as I had done twice already, I motioned for the table to lean in close. "I'm sorry." I spoke as loud as I dared. "I'm from Texas and have nothing to write with. Yesterday I was..." I started to say "captured" but changed my mind. "*Brought* here out of the desert, and I know nothing about any of this or where I am, actually. Would someone please loan me writing materials?"

No one budged. Everyone stared with blank, joyless expressions. Never had I seen such lifeless eyes. They all seemed to not have laughed in ages, if ever. The glum looks gave me an idea. Weren't they an audience? A tough one but still an audience. And how long had I been preparing for just such an occasion—not exactly like this for sure, but still—to perform? Had all my stand-up routines at the Joke Shop back home where I'd practiced performing in front of live audiences been wasted? Had the untold hours doing impressions before a mirror and throwing my voice been for nothing? Was I a ventriloquist, or not? And what had the founder of the Joke Shop, who in his day had written lines for such legends as Edgar Bergen, drummed into my head before going on stage—"Grab their interest to start or bomb."

After a deep, bracing inhale and slow, nerve-settling exhale, I extended my right arm to the center of the table and made a puppet of my fist. "Pssst! Guys?" By moving my thumb up and down for a bottom lip, my fist turned into a mouth. "Hey, fellows? Look'it here!"

Those at the table looked at my hand, then up at my mouth, then back to my hand, and finally to my mouth again. One or two smiles broke out. Such a feeling of relief came over me that I had to really focus. My audience hadn't been won over yet. "My name's Pepe." That had been the stage name for my puppet at the Joke Shop. "My friend needs a pen and paper, please."

All eyes stared at my hand puppet. A single giggle from among the onlookers proved the inspiration I needed. "My friend forgot to bring something to write with."

The neighbor to my left, the one who shunned me first, bent down for a closer look. He was about my age, although his shoulders came to my eye level. His face had rough, leathery skin. A tic kept bunching one cheek, tugging his upper lip and partly opening that corner of his mouth. Just as it seemed there'd be no reaction, he looked over and his face lit up. His whole personality changed with that smile. I heaved a silent sigh.

Encouraged, I extended my third and fourth fingers and, while using my thumb and index finger for a mouth, strutted the hand puppet back and forth across the table as best I could. Smothered laughter came from every direction, which pleased me as much as a standing ovation.

A red-haired fellow across the table motioned everyone to lean in close. For a second, I resented the intrusion, worried he might be hogging the limelight. "El Ciempies," he murmured, pointing at my puppet. This brought on repressed snickers.

Not until then did I realize the figure *did* look like Centipede. His long-legged strut, his being all mouth, and his having no head to speak of made the puppet a dead ringer. Because of this, I used my little finger as best I could to cross my puppet's chest in a Roman-style salute as the lanky leader had done and breathed a quiet, "Ahhh-aha-ahaaa!"

This really broke everyone up. I became so absorbed in the fun I forgot who might be standing within easy viewing range. Some in the audience stifled laughter behind their hands, while others, with shoulders quaking, buried their heads in their arms atop the table. To my great delight, several elbowed their neighbors, increasing the number of on-lookers. I was a hit, if I did say so myself. Such a bounty of pencils and pa-per appeared in front of me that, if Centipede weren't around, I would've jumped up and shouted for joy.

However, the next moment everything tanked. The room darkened, and my small audience turned away one by one until all faced the pro-jector screen. The reason for their lost interest, besides the film begin-ning, could only be one thing—the novelty had worn off. Anyone who'd studied the entertainment business for very long had read about the "Comedian's Curse." Those who couldn't come up with fresh jokes were doomed. Every book on the subject warned about the letdown and re-sulting depression that followed the Comedian's Curse. Unless prepared for beforehand, many a comic sunk into despair and a career-ending loss of sense of humor. Thankfully, the film started, sparing me from the dis-appointment. After the thrill I'd just experienced, though, who could pay attention? Not me, unfortunately.

The film finished at last, but before I could set up to perform again everyone at the tables stood. This time, unlike their orderly entrance into the mess hall, they left as a milling mob. I tried to show the last stragglers my puppet trick, but they acted in too big a rush. Consequently, I ended up one of the last ones out the door.

In no hurry and still relishing my recent triumph, I stood under an awning at the top of a short staircase, overlooking the trailers, the ghost town and the water tower with the sloppily painted death's-head. Down below in a dirt yard, three square formations had already assembled, each composed of four lines.

That's when it hit me. The sight brought to mind my predicament. Where to go? No one had told me. Either that, or else the film had given instruc-tions and I failed to pay attention. A cold dread spread over me. From where I stood, no open spaces appeared in the even lines of bodies.

I hurried down the steps. The afternoon sun, after the shade, felt like going under a launch pad where a rocket was blasting off. Reflections from shiny objects pricked my eyes, while patches of shade, rare as they were, looked as inviting as cave openings.

The assembly stood at attention. Our buckskin-outfitted leader paced back and forth in front of everyone, appearing the picture of impatience. I hunched down behind the last line, still searching for a gap to fill, but was unable to find an opening. The view between the lines of recruits went all the way to the front. Our lanky leader had stopped pacing. His tiny head with its quick eyes rotated mantis-like. How long could I go on without being noticed? Should I try to sneak back into the mess hall? But how to get up the stairs without being seen? I almost wished the earth would open up and swallow me. As expected, those two beady eyes locked onto the one out-of-place oddity.

Centipede cocked his miniature head as if unable to understand at first, but then his pimply face reddened and jutted forward. He shrieked a cry like some awful parrot and stabbed a finger at the ground in front of him. Left with no choice, I crept forward, cringing and shivering with every step, barely able to keep my legs underneath me while stammering an apology.

Centipede made a sweeping gesture with his hand, but I couldn't stop. He had to understand that my disruption hadn't been on purpose.

The small-headed leader charged forward as if to run me down. I shrank back, covering my head, but thankfully no blows came.

"Fifty sit-ups!" he yelled down on my head.

I peeked out from under one arm, uncertain I heard right. Fifty? Did he say "fifty?" But I can't do that many. I'd never done so much as one. "I'm sorry, but—"

"Sixty!"

Sixty? That's even worse. As I stared, his furious face bobbed up and down, which seemed strange until I realized my own trembling was the cause. "N-No, pardon, but—"

"Seventy!"

Impossible! This was getting out of hand. What was needed was for everyone to take a deep breath. "H—Hold on, let me ex—"

"Eighty!"

"Oh, really, that's out of the question. I'd never be able—"

"Ninety!"

"Please, listen, won't you? I'm out of shape. A weakling, really, who c—"

"One hundred. *More?*"

I wondered what the chances of going back to fifty were. It didn't take an Einstein to know better than to ask. Maybe if I showed him I couldn't do it, he'd be satisfied? So I dropped to my knees. The sand's heat burned through my jeans and stung me despite my shirt as I stretched out onto my back. After crossing my hands over my chest, I twisted through every contortion imaginable to accomplish eleven sit-ups. Exhausted, I fell back and squinted at a bright sun straight above, hoping by some miracle the effort would make him happy.

A narrow shade overshadowed me, blocking the sun. Directly above, a small face exactly fit the orange ball in the sky and outlined his shrunken head in a fiery halo. He bent down close. With a calloused finger, he lifted my chin, tilting my head back into the sand.

"In thirty days, you'll do two hundred sit-ups, two hundred squat-thrusts, duck-walk one-hundred meters, and run fifteen kilometers with a pack—all before breakfast. You'll read and study at night and learn what we teach perfectly." He snorted. "You stay here today. Tonight, too. No water. Tomorrow you do one hundred sit-ups or stay the next day and night." Before leaving, he chucked me under the chin with a painful scrape of his rough finger. "Now, prac—tice."

The bad-tempered leader left, followed by all the others. With every-one gone, I let go a long, slow, emptying sigh. Doing a hundred sit-ups might as well be a thousand. In case Centipede still watched, though, I laid unmoving except for my twitching stomach muscles. After lick-ing sand off my chapped lips, I tried sit-ups again, this time reaching twelve. An improvement, but still a long way to go. I tried once more.

Twenty-one, but on the last three I cheated by pushing off with one hand. Was it even possible for someone who had never done so much as one sit-up to do a hundred within twenty-four hours? Doubtful. Very doubtful. Sure enough, the next try I only made it to ten before collapsing, my worst effort yet. No, I'd been wrong before. Not a thousand sit-ups, more like ten thousand.

As I lay there grieving over the hopelessness of the task, only one question occupied my mind. How in the world did I ever get myself into such a mess?

CHAPTER 2
The First Ms.

~

HAD IT ONLY BEEN TWO weeks ago? Only fourteen days since I'd been safe in my own bed, able to sleep as late as I liked with no worries? It seemed a lifetime ago even though I could remember it like yesterday. I'd awakened around noon with that same pesky phrase going over and over in my mind like a chalkboard punishment at school.

"Bad habits are light sleepers. Bad habits are light sleepers. Bad habits are light sleepers."

Why my mother's favorite saying picked that particular moment to torment me, who knew, but how true nonetheless. Bad habits do wake up easy, and they're stronger the second time. In the days when Hect and I had been on the run, I'd gotten up before first light. Now safe and once again in my own bed, I hadn't seen the sun until it was straight overhead at high noon. Laziness had slipped up on me sly as a germ. Not only that, but even after almost twelve hours of sleep I barely had energy at all, and yet when I'd been on the run with Hect we never slowed down.

Speaking of Hect, where had my best friend ended up? Was he still alive? If so, what would he being doing at this moment? Had he and Ju made it to the place called the "camp." whatever that was, after they left me stranded in the desert? And come to think of it, how could they abandon me after I fell off the truck? I could understand Ju leaving me as we'd just met in the Juarez jail, but why had my best friend not come back? They may have assumed I'd been killed by the fall, but couldn't they come back and check? Except for a miracle, I would have died, too. A knock on my bedroom door interrupted my thoughts.

"It's almost noon, Sleepyhead," Mother called through my bedroom door. "Are you up?"

"No, I'm still in bed."

"I'm coming in."

"I'm not dressed."

"You knew last night we had this meeting scheduled this afternoon." She paused for a suspenseful moment. "Didn't you say when you got home you had changed; that from now on you'd get up early and get busy? Whatever became of that young, energetic ball of fire? Bad habits are light sleepers, you know."

"Yeah, yeah, spare me. I haven't been home long enough yet. I'm still catching up on my sleep."

"Well, put some clothes on—something dressy. Pretend we're all going to brunch at the country club."

That should've been my first clue to trouble ahead. Why dress up? For what? As a last hope, I tried one more delaying tactic. "How about we meet later on? Not now."

"She can't." My bedroom door slowly opened. Mother looked unsure at first, but then brightened. She was still pretty, despite her weight. Her soft blue eyes, though tired, hadn't lost their sparkle, but, as usual, her smile dominated her whole face. "Well, well, look who's sitting up in bed. That's a start. Good morning."

"I already have plans." I didn't, of course, but it was all I could think of.

"I said good morning."

"Morning, morning. This afternoon would be a better time." A lie, of course, as I had no intention of coming back once out of here.

"It *is* this afternoon. You've wasted half the day again. Where do you have to go that you can't meet right now?"

"To..." I had to think fast. "To find someone who might help me find Hect."

"Not that again," she said with a sigh. "Every morning it's the same thing. Why do we have to go through this over and over?"

She was right. I had been putting off finding my friend. Somebody needed to help Hect, but who? He had no family to speak of, just an uncle and aunt, but they were too crippled and poor to hire anyone. Then who else? Me, of course, if I had one ounce of decency. But the idea of making the long trek across west Texas, navigating that massive city of Juarez, and recrossing the Mexican desert filled me with dismay. And yet the guilt of forsaking my best friend gnawed at me. As a compromise, I settled for worrying, and talking about rescuing him every day, and doing nothing. I had no shortage of excuses either. How could someone small like me make it all the way to Mexico? Or, where, in that endless wasteland, should I start looking for the camp that Ju had been taking us to? If I could figure out the answer to those, I'd come up with more lame reasons, but not about to admit to any of that, I had to say something. "Yeah, but this time I mean it."

"Over my dead body, young man. You'll never go back to Mexico, not if I have anything to do with it. Don't you realize by now how dangerous that place is?"

"Someone has to. His aunt and uncle can't. If they had any money, they might hire someone, but they're penniless. Would you want me to just abandon him?"

"You're not going, and that's final. Why argue about it? To tell the truth, you and I both know you have no intention of going. If I thought for one minute you were the least bit serious, I'd lock you in your bedroom and throw away the key." She smiled as if we shared a secret. "Why don't you just admit it? You don't really want to go, do you?"

That hurt, but she had me on that one. Down deep, did I really even *want* to go help my best friend? Weren't all my protests really just put on to keep from facing the fact that, like everyone else, I didn't care enough?

"I thought so." She smiled. "Now we can forget all this silliness. We'll expect you out in the den in five minutes. The three of us have some important items to discuss that involve your future."

Another telling clue went by unnoticed. Had I been paying attention, I might have anticipated what lay ahead and made a run for it out the back door. Instead, I kept up the same useless stall. "You two go ahead without me. I'll agree to whatever you decide." Another dodge, but it was all I had. "You and that woman—"

"Not 'that woman'—**Ms.** Dronaman. I don't know why you won't call her by her right name. Pardon my interrupting like that, but it's important. She's my dearest friend."

"Okay, Mrs.—"

"Not, Mrs. Ms."

"Miss—"

"No, shorten the *s* sound. *Ms.* Now you try."

"What's the big deal?"

"It's new. European, actually, from the seventeenth century. Back in those times, 'mistress' was a popular term to call single women and didn't imply the bad reputation of today. She shortened it to Ms."

"Why?"

"It's different, don't you think?"

"So's goathead."

"Very funny." She didn't laugh, though. "Anyway, what's the crime? She didn't want to be thought of like everyone else so she researched it, as she does everything, and came up with 'Ms.' She just wants to be known as an independent, self-reliant woman and feels her marital status is nobody else's business."

"You mean that she's been divorced six times?"

"Timmy!" she gasped, glancing over her shoulder. "What on earth's the matter with you? How many times she's been married is none of your business, or anyone else's for that matter. Besides, I told you that tidbit in the strictest confidence. Now I wish I'd never told you at all."

"Aw, she can't hear way out there."

"Anyway," she said in a calmer tone, "how many times she's been married has nothing to do with it. It's not like when…"

She kept talking, but I was too upset to listen. Oh, what made me sleep late? Now look at the jam I was in. Was I born lazy? Did I inherit this no-get-up-and-go? I had so much more energy when the day began early. Starting out at noon left me not only weary but with barely an appetite. Back when I worked at the Pines Diner in New Mexico, rest happened from midnight to first light, and I'd gobbled scraps off customers' plates like every meal was my last. Now, with twice the sleep, I had half the drive.

"Timmy!" Mother called, scattering my thoughts. "Are you listening? You've got that blank stare again. Oh, well..." She stood to her feet with some exertion. All the time I'd been away in Mexico she'd gotten even heavier. "I can't keep company waiting. Get your clothes on and come out to the den."

I started to protest, but she held a hand up. "No excuses." She walked toward the door but, evidently having a last thought, stopped short. "Put on a freshly ironed shirt, pressed slacks, and a tie. Make sure everything matches, no clashing. Show us some of that Collins class our family is so famous for." She giggled.

The two women sat in sofa chairs at opposite ends of an oval, glass-topped coffee table. When I entered the den all talk ceased, which only amplified the racket my clothes made. My jeans flapped at the ripped knees, the safety pins holding my buttonless shirt together jangled, and the sole of one tennis shoe slapped as the tape had lost its stickum.

One look and Mother spit her coffee back into her cup. After a choking spell, she cleared her throat. "Why—why, Timmy," she called gaily. "Can you say hello, please?"

"Sure. Hi'ya."

"Hello, Timothy," Ms. Dronaman replied stiffly.

I winced at the name. She's the only one who ever called me that. How would she like it if I called her Ms. Dronamaney? The woman had long auburn hair to her shoulders and a freckled, narrow face with bottle-cap eyes that, if they'd been any closer together, would have made her a Cyclops.

"Timothy could be such a cosmopolitan young man," she said to Mother, "with some effort, of course. He's certainly got all the advantages—good looks, a slim build, straight posture, when he doesn't slouch, and such charisma when he enters a room that he draws everyone's attention. If only he'd make use of those assets one day."

Sunshine poured through a row of picture windows, spilling over the couch and pooling in puddles of light at the women's feet. The thick, bright green carpet blended with the yellow, blue, and red pattern that covered all the furniture.

The two women looked at me expectantly. Judging by the lengthening silence, it was my turn to talk, but what to say? What else but the old standby my mother taught me to ask a man about his work and compliment a woman. "Your hair's nice, *Ms*. Dronaman. It makes her look younger, don't you think, Mother?"

The freckled woman responded in pleasurable tones, but I had other things on my mind, mainly my mother's oddly struggling face. With her head cocked over to one side, she mouthed something over and over.

"Th…Th…*Thanks*…for the…for the…" Reading Mother's lips proved difficult. "Com…ugh…pli…*Compliment*. That's it!"

Mother's face relaxed.

"Sit here," Ms. Dronaman insisted. "I want you seated next to me."

I looked around the room for anywhere to sit besides there. A piano bench at the far end of the room had about the right distance but would provoke a scene. A barstool at the counter separating the kitchen might have worked if it hadn't faced the wrong way.

"Here!" she persisted and patted a cushion on the couch nearest her. "Sit down, I insist."

After a last longing look around the room, my situation seemed hopeless.

"Timothy, don't hesitate. It's a sign of weak character. I told you where to sit, now sit here!" She patted the couch cushion nearest her. "Here's a spot."

"Dog pee, I bet."

She lifted her hand and stared at the cushion.

"Timmy!" Mother exclaimed. "He's only kidding. Aren't you kidding, Timmy?"

"I'm only kidding."

"He's always teasing." Mother laughed, but not in a way that invited us to join in. "I wish he'd be more serious, but I try to understand. After all, I tell myself, he wants to be an entertainer one day, what with his ventriloquism and stand-up routines. He's doing the best he can at his age to relate to other people, I suppose."

Left with no choice, I sat in the middle of the couch, equal distance from the two women. Feeling cornered, I picked up a throw pillow and tossed it into the air and caught it over and over.

"Stop that, dear," Mother said, reaching over and patting my knee.

I put the pillow down, but without thinking picked it up again and threw it into the air and caught it. Mother frowned.

"He's hungry," Ms. Dronaman offered.

"There's leftover steak from last night," Mother said to me. "See what you missed by not showing up for dinner?" She turned to Ms. Dronaman. "When Timmy doesn't get home till late, I'm left to fend for myself, what with his father, well—" she winked, "—*away.*"

What had that been about? Did she think I didn't know my father was at one of his drying out centers? Or else, could it be that not everyone knew about his drinking? Was it a family secret? Who knew?

"For instance," Mother continued, "last night I dined all by myself at the Chuck Wagon Steak House."

I saw my chance. Somebody had to lighten things up. "'Make yourself happy,'" I sang, repeating the radio ad jingle, "'Chuck Wagon's service is snappy.'"

Neither woman laughed.

Not about to be discouraged, I made my fist into a puppet and, using my thumb for a bottom lip as I'd done many times at the Joke Shop, sang the entire radio ad through "Pepe," my hand puppet, without moving my lips. Another flop.

"Timothy," Ms. Dronaman observed dryly, "that's cute, I'm sure, among your little friends, but this is an adult discussion we're having here."

"Sorry, Timmy," Mother added. "Save the ventriloquism for another venue."

"Okay, enough of that," Ms. Dronaman put in. "Timothy, your mother and I want you to understand why you have to go through what we're planning for you."

That got my attention. Alerted to a plot afoot, I picked up the pillow and played catch again. On my third toss, Mother lunged from her chair, caught the pillow in midair, and placed it next to her.

"Don't worry," Ms. Dronaman observed, speaking to my mother. "It will be difficult at first, but Timothy will adjust. He'll do well, in time."

On high alert now, I was all ears.

"I'm so proud of you, Timmy," Mother said. "After all, this is for your own good."

If whatever they were planning was "for my own good," I wanted no part of it. Was this what I got for putting off going to find Hect? I sure wished my best friend were here now. Things always worked out with him around. Without him, I felt helpless. Not only that, but what if our positions had been reversed? What if, instead of me falling off the truck, he'd been the one to take a tumble and then made his way out of the desert? Would he delay rescuing me? How would I feel if he took his sweet time?

Mother patted my leg, startling me. "Did you hear what Ms. Dronaman asked?"

"Oh, sure." A lie, of course, but how to help it? "Every word."

"Well?"

"Well, what?"

"*Well?*" she said irritably. "She asked you a question. Since she's with the school administration, she wants to know if you're complying with the curfew. As she just got through explaining, with that crazy man having escaped from Big Spring State Mental Hospital, everyone fifteen and under must be off the streets by eleven o'clock. She asked you twice what time you got home last night."

"I'm not sure, Ms. Dronaman, I was too bombed to notice."

"Oh, dear!" Mother cried. "You've spilled your coffee, you poor thing. Here, let me get a cloth."

"No, no, I'm fine, I'm fine." The woman blotted her lap with a napkin. "Sit down, please, I'm all right."

"But, really, he's kidding again. Aren't you kidding, Timmy?"

"I'm kidding. It's just a joke."

"Oh, yes, I see," Ms. Dronaman said, crushing her napkin in a tight fist. "It's that outlandish sense of humor of yours again. So, it's your ambition to be a comic, is it? In that case, you really must learn the truth about the paid jesters of today. They're actually frightened underneath it all. Comedy is a disguise timid people hide behind because they have little courage, so they make fun of everything, usually in a demeaning way. But comedians never develop any solid character, sadly, for always hiding behind jokes."

I squirmed.

She leaned forward in her chair to within inches of my face, her eyes set so close together they merged into a double yoke. "Let me inform you of what your mother and I were really discussing before your entry into the room."

Her pinched smile reminded me of the attorney in the movies who at the last minute finds the missing clue to amaze the jury and doom the defendant.

"Your mother and I agree that because of your behavior lately you simply must be taken in hand. Innocent mischief is one thing, but it's quite another to have been guilty of the delinquent acts you committed before fleeing to Mexico—burning down a building in a junkyard, shooting guns off, drinking beer, running from the law, and ending up in a Juarez jail. Such antics must stop. Just because you were lucky enough to solve a crime with such misbehavior and earn an award from an insurance company of a few thousand dollars is no excuse. What is needed here is an authority figure to exert control and some good old-fashioned discipline. You're going to military school, young man. The George S. Patton."

"She's kidding, isn't she, Mother?"

"No, Timmy, she's not."

CHAPTER 3
The Adult Discussion

IT'S NOT EASY TO KEEP a straight face when life collapses around you in two of the most awful words ever created—*military school!* And not just any military school either. Every kid who'd ever gotten into a scrape had been threatened with the George S. Patton Military Academy in Kerrville, Texas. Troublemakers from all over the state ended up there and, from the rumors, the place more resembled an army boot camp than anything to do with school.

Despite feeling as if I'd just been knocked for a double backflip, I knew that this was no time to lose control. Level heads must prevail. By not reacting, I hoped to throw them off.

"You don't say? Well, fancy that. The George S. Patton, hmm? Well, well." If I could only remain cool and collected between now and time to pack up and leave, there'd be plenty of chances to change Mother's mind. As soon as Cyclops got out of the way, I'd go to work, but for now I'd have to play along. "In that case, I look forward to attending next spring."

"You leave this afternoon, Timmy," Mother said, dropping another A-bomb. "I've already registered you. I'll pack your things. You start classes tomorrow first thing."

Compared to the last shock, which hadn't been minor by any means, the needle on this one went off the scale. I couldn't think. I tried to speak, but my brain had locked down. The words wouldn't come.

"Timothy?" Ms. Dronaman added, perhaps noticing my stumped reaction. "This was my doing, not your mother's, who at this point doesn't know what to do with you. If you blame anyone, blame me. It's my decision that you need a fresh start—a brand new beginning, new acquaintances, but most of all, you require discipline in your life."

"I did agree, though," Mother added. "Still, I feel bad, mostly because I want to take you there myself. But it's impossible at the moment because of your father. They want me to be part of his counseling. However, I'll make the trip to Kerrville in a few days."

"I'm taking you to school, Timothy," Ms. Dronaman announced. "You and I can drive down together. I'll finish registering you and take care of any paperwork. On the way, we can spend the trip having a little talk about manhood, you and I. It'll be fun."

I tried to speak, but the words stuck in my throat.

"I don't think she heard you, Timmy," Mother said. "Can you say thank you for going to all the trouble to drive you to Kerrville and registering you in school?"

"Um…urk. Gawk."

"You're welcome, Timothy," she said, although how she understood the strangled reply was beyond me. "I'm glad to help your mother out."

"Good," Mother said as if that settled it. "I'll pack his things." She turned toward me. "I just know you're going to do so well, Timmy. A military man, my, my. You'll look so sharp in your starched uniform, sporting a tie and wearing polished dress shoes for a change."

That did it! Unable to take any more, I bounded to my feet. Ms. Dronaman pushed back in her chair, looking fearful of what might happen next.

"What in the world?" Mother gasped.

"I have something…or, I have to do…er…" It all came clear in a sudden burst of insight. "If I'm leaving today, I've got something I *have* to do. Right away. It can't wait."

"For goodness' sake, what is it, Timmy?"

"To the bank!"

"The bank?" Her smile faded. "Why the bank, of all places?"

"To draw out half the insurance money."

"Oh, no, you don't." She squinted so thin her eyes disappeared. "You're not about to touch that money, Timmy Collins. Just because you're going to military school, don't think you're going to take a big pile of cash along. No, sir! Not on your life. Everything's taken care of. I'll send you an allowance for spending money. That insurance reward is for college, I already told you."

"Not my money. *Hect's!* His money."

"Oh, him. Why? Legally, it's none of his. The insurance company paid you, not him. You're the one who uncovered the fraud as far as they're concerned. Besides, who knows where he ended up? He may be gone for good for all anyone knows."

"Half of it's still his money. I can't keep it. That'd be stealing. Besides, his family needs it. His uncle can't work anymore, and they barely get by. With me away at military school, he won't be able to get to his share if he comes back. I'll take his half over to his uncle for safekeeping."

She harrumphed. "I don't know why you ever ran around with that boy in the first place. Whoever heard of dropping out of school in the seventh grade?"

"Maybe he'll go back." I felt the argument shifting my way. "Plus the fact, now that the family has money, maybe they'll be able to locate him in Mexico and get him home."

"The bank's not going to hand over a thousand dollars to a fifteen year old, even if the account is in your name."

"They will if you call ahead and okay it."

"Me?"

"Why not? Everyone in town knows the story anyway. The insurance reward for the dress shop burning down is the biggest thing to happen around here. If you tell them I'm taking my friend's share to him, they'll do it."

"Okay, I'll call. Only, as soon as you give the money to his uncle, you come straight back here. We've lots to do to get ready."

"They live south of town across the tracks in a trailer court. It'll take an hour or so. And no checks. Cash only." In all my worrying about finding my friend and planning how I should rescue him, I'd thought everything out beforehand. "They're so poor they don't even own a bank account."

"All right, but you be sure not to drop it on the way. Meanwhile, I'll get you packed for your trip. There's a ton of things to think about."

On my way out, Mother cleared her throat in that special way to let me know I'd forgotten something.

"Good-bye, Ms. Dronaman." I called in response before closing the front door. "Sorry we didn't get a chance to visit longer, although when you think about it, the visit *was* pretty long." After the door shut, I cupped my mouth. "Just kidding."

The shortcut to A Street crossed the fairway of the Midland Country Club golf course. Four old guys on the tee box shouted at me, but I ran too fast to make out what they said. After circling the fifteenth green, where three lady golfers stopped putting to glare at me, I crossed A Street, climbed a wire fence, sprinted through the graveyard, turned up Big Spring Avenue, and, after three intersections, arrived at the tall buildings downtown. All in all, the shortcut saved six blocks.

Catty-corner to the Shell Tower, the tallest building in town, the First National Bank looked like something out of a Randolph Scott Western. With real swinging saloon doors, spittoons, and a brass foot rail that ran along beneath barred teller cages, chaps and spurs seemed more in style than the business suits the men wore. A lady teller conferred with a heavyset man before handing me an envelope. I signed a paper that contained who knows what kind of information.

"I'm Harvey Watson," the heavyset man behind the teller said through window bars. "Your mom called and said for me to be sure and warn you to put that away in a safe place and don't take it out until you get where it belongs."

"Yes, sir." I drew my shoulders up, trying to look responsible. "And thanks."

Once outside again, I was too scared to open the envelope until around the corner from the bank and into the entryway of the not-yet-open Yucca movie theater. I counted ten hundred-dollar bills. A thousand bucks. I'd never handled even close to that much money before in my entire life. The wealthiest oilman in Midland couldn't have felt any richer.

The idea of returning home and packing a bag crossed my mind, but it involved too much risk. I needed a change of clothes bad, especially because the sole of my tennis shoe kept folding under, but anything could go wrong. Besides, my travels so far had been without luggage; why start dragging around a suitcase now?

At the Greyhound bus station, as luck would have it, the last bus to El Paso left ten minutes before. The next one went to San Angelo, which took me south instead of west, but at least it got me out of town. When I didn't show up back home, people would start looking, and I'd better be as far away as possible. If there wasn't a bus to El Paso from San Angelo, I could always get out on the highway and hitchhike.

On the bus station counter sat a rack of postcards with three-cent stamps already on them. While waiting, I wrote a letter.

> *Dear Dad and Mom, by the time you get this, you'll have figured out I'm not going to military school. Hect's out in the desert of Mexico, and I can't leave him there. He's my best friend, even if you don't approve of him, and he needs my help. Don't notify the cops in Juarez unless you want me to go to prison. Hect and I escaped from the Juarez jail, and they'll arrest me. I have friends in Mexico who will help. As soon as I find him, I'll bring him back and that's a promise. I hope you're not mad because I believe it's the right thing to do.*
> *Tim*

After dropping the card in the postal drop box on the street, I realized I hadn't signed off with "Love," but it was too late now. My bus had arrived.

CHAPTER 4

Back to Juarez

On the bus ride from Midland to San Angelo, the scenery changed dramatically at the midway point. Instead of miles and miles of sand, scruffy mesquite, pump jacks, and oil derrick sludge pits belching up black smoke entwined with orange flame, we drove into flattop plateaus. From my point of view, we'd left the flatlands and arrived in the Rockies. After a stop in the frontier-looking town of San Angelo, the bus kept on south, but I got off and waited for one heading west. With a two-hour stopover before one left for El Paso, I found a steakhouse. A T-bone with all the trimmings, plus apple pie a la mode and a nice big tip for the waiter hardly made a dent in one of my hundred-dollar bills. A shopping spree became the next order of business. I bought jeans, two shirts, socks, underwear, a pair of loafers, plus a travel bag. I left my old clothes on the fitting room floor. At Walgreens, I bought a toothbrush and comb and such.

Back at the bus station, it took the last cash of my first hundred to buy a ticket to Big Spring, Van Horn, Sierra Blanca, and then El Paso, but I still had nine more in my sock inside my shoe. What's to worry about? On my first trip to Mexico, I had fifteen dollars. Compared to that, I traveled like the richest oil tycoon.

Of all the odd twists of fate, the trip meant retracing the very route I'd just made. Although we returned to Midland, we didn't stop there. Still, the bus ride to San Angelo hadn't been a complete waste. At least I'd avoided bumping into a family friend or being seen hanging around the

Midland bus stop. Just to be on the safe side, though, when we passed through my hometown, I stayed in the bus restroom.

After Midland, every mile we traveled along Highway 80 brought back memories from my first trip to Mexico—the place where the sheriff's dog, Mauler, got hit by the '48 Chevy, the railroad tracks Hect and I slept next to when the supposed "UFO" train went speeding past, the spot where we parted company to begin hitchhiking, then the place my friend passed me in that convertible Thunderbird with the St. Bernard, and finally the highway intersection I'd taken north to New Mexico. After going under the overpass, I connected scenes to events Hect told me about—where he met up with T.J. the trucker, and his beautiful-but-backstabbing daughter, Becca; the fruit stand they'd stopped at to buy cantaloupes; the town of Pecos, where the three pulled the scam called the Poison Log Routine; and the highway cafe at Sierra Blanca, which sold T. J. his first bottles of gin. Later on, we passed the most significant place of all, the truck stop across the highway from where Eli picked me up and tried to get me to join his criminal gang. Because of all the sights, the eight-hour bus ride went by in no time at all.

Once we reached El Paso, I walked to the International Bridge and from there to the bus terminal in Juarez. The shabby building had such rusted-out wrecks parked out front that you'd have to be on your last resort like me to ride one. No one spoke English, of course, so they couldn't understand what I meant when I described the town I wanted to go to. After all the time I'd spent in Mexico, I'd never gotten used to how isolated our two countries had become from each other though they were only a stone's-throw apart. Next, I tried taxis, but the few drivers who got the idea of where my friends Bernardo and Maria lived declined to take me, no doubt on account of the poor roads.

Frustrated at every turn, I had nevertheless committed too much to give up. What was the alternative anyway? Go home? Endure a ride to military school with the likes of the Cyclops lecturing me? And what about Hect? Should I leave him to whatever trouble or danger he might be in?

No, not likely. It just wasn't in me to throw in the towel on my best friend that easily. There had to be some other way.

While wandering the crowded streets and poking my head in and out of shops, I eavesdropped on every conversation, hoping to find someone speaking English. Was there not one person in this city of millions who could talk to me? Come to think of it, why would anyone speak English when everyone else spoke Spanish? The only reason they'd switch was if they wanted something from an American. The thought stopped me short.

Of course, why hadn't I thought of it before? Someone *did* speak English. The flat-faced, street girl with the pug nose who'd stood in the doorway on my first trip to Juarez. I'd met her, and we'd talked a little right before I found Hect and Becca. She'd been able to speak at least a bare minimum of English, enough to call out to me. And there'd been a park across the street from where she stood, one of this city's very few that I'd come across.

After that I asked everyone the same one-word question, "Park?" "Park?" "Park?" Finally, a shopkeeper pointed up the street while holding up three fingers, which I took to mean as many blocks.

With nighttime approaching, I found the park. Sure enough, the girl stood across the street in a doorway. Her face looked even flatter than before, with a pug nose like a bullet had hit dead center in a pie pan. She wore the same tiny skirt, or one similar, over wide hips, exposing turkey-drumstick thighs and calves. I never before felt so glad to see someone.

"Hey, hello!" I dodged smoking taxis until safely across the street. "Remember me?"

Her engraved smile came to life. She nodded enthusiastically.

I thought it best to let her know right off my intentions. "Can we talk?"

She looked puzzled.

"Talk, you know. Talk?" I stayed down at street level while she stood atop a three-step staircase, looking to me like an angel, even if a fallen one.

"Si."

"Um, hi, what's happening?" It was all I could think of. How could I find out if conversation was even possible? "How are you?"

She nodded. "*Bien.*"

Enough of that. Time to get down to basics. "I wish to...um..." Let's see, how to describe what I wanted? "A small town...No, a tiny town... No, a village."

"Pueblo?"

Ah-ha, progress. We'd made contact. I pointed out toward the desert. "Pueblo. Ten miles or so." I held up all fingers of both hands. "A pueblo?"

"San Miguel?"

Who knew? There must be a dozen such tiny towns. If only there was something special about it, something unique. Then I had it. In the sand covering the sidewalk, I drew a trunk with a huge round ball on top and a tiny square house next to it. "A tree. The biggest tree around. In fact, the *only* tree around. Half-dead, but very big."

She beamed and, because of it, her face became less homely. "Si. La casa de mi tio."

She had me on that one. I stood and shook my head.

"Mi tio," she repeated, as if saying it twice should clear things up. "San Miguel. Mi tio."

Still having no idea, I shrugged.

"Mi tio, Victor."

Bingo! I could hardly believe my ears. But could there be two of them? "Victor? You know Victor? I know Victor. We met on my first trip to Juarez."

She nodded. "Mi tio."

"Tio—Tio, is that *friend*?" Oh, what's the matter with me? *Amigo* is friend. I knew better than that. "So Victor is your...?"

"Tio."

Back to where we started. Maybe if I tried another route. "Truck. Pickup with many colors underneath the big tree."

She brightened even more. "Si, mi tio."

No use going over that again. Time to start guessing. "Is 'tio' your dad? Papá?"

She shook her head and held up two fingers side by side, as if a pair.

"Father's brother! Your *uncle*!"

She clapped, and I realized she could understand more English than she spoke. "So then, Victor's your uncle, or tio, who lives in the house with the big tree and owns the many-colored truck. Well, fancy that."

She nodded excitedly.

"Victor gave me a ride." Even though she didn't understand it all, I kept talking, hoping something would register. "Can you get word to him for me? A note. A message." I pretended to write on the palm of my hand. "Tell him to come here to me. I need him. Come here and help me."

"Bien," she said, appearing to grasp some at least.

It occurred to me that with her being from such a small town, smaller even than the one I grew up in, that if she knew one person, she probably knew them all. It was worth a try. "Bernardo? Ber-nar-do, do you know Maria and Bernardo?"

"Si, si, Bernardo." She nodded vigorously. "Bernardo es mi padre."

This was too much. "Your *father*? No kidding."

She wagged her head, indicating wrong answer; then clasped her hands under her chin as the villagers had done at dinner that day on my first trip to Mexico after the mules brought me out of the desert. As unlikely as it seemed, her position could only mean one thing.

"Prayer? Bernardo's your preacher? You can't be serious."

"Si, mi padre."

Considering how she earned her living, there had to be a story worth hearing about behind that one, but we had no time now. "Okay, tell Victor and Bernardo to come." I pointed down at my feet. "Here! Quick, quick! I'll pay." I patted my front pocket, even though all the money was in my sock.

Judging by her bouncing enthusiasm, she got the point, but something bothered me. With no telephone poles around, how could anyone get a message to a town out in the desert? Even in Victor's pickup, it had taken us most of a day to make the trip. Then again, what other choice did I have?

She waved me inside. Once through the doorway, I took one look and the shock hit me faster than I could cover up. She noticed, too, because from then on she avoided making eye contact. The only furniture in the room was a swayback bed, sunk deep as a hammock. There were no chairs, tables, pictures on the walls, or anything that made the place look homey. Just four blank walls. Beneath the thin, drooping mattress, a number-four washtub was used for no-telling-what—a bathtub or maybe worse. If I'd gone a month without sleep, I wouldn't stretch out on that bed.

The girl motioned me to stay put, which she needn't have. I had no desire to take a step farther. On her way out the back door, she stopped as if having an afterthought. "Cinco?" She held up five fingers.

"Yes, yes. Five dollars. More, if you hurry." The price seemed steep to deliver a message, but then again, with no telephones, getting word to another town had to be no small chore. Anyway, what was one five-dollar bill compared to my stockpile?

Not until that moment did it hit me. After the girl left, I hurriedly took my shoe off and got my nest egg out of my sock. Sure enough, all hundreds. Nine of them. But who around here could break a hundred? I'd spent the other one on bus fares, food, and clothes, leaving me for all practical purposes flat broke. My great idea for carrying cash in the smallest bundle backfired. Now how could I pay the girl? Should I go from shop to shop asking for change? Into what—pesos? At twelve to one, that'd be a thousand-two-hundred pesos just for one hundred-dollar bill. Besides that, if and when Bernardo and Victor got here, no telling who might come with them, and I could just see myself fumbling around with hundred-dollar bills in front of strangers.

With nothing working out as planned so far, I sat on my heels, exhausted to my very bones, and leaned back against the wall. Once things got quiet, dark lumps in the shadows moved amid scratching noises. Rats! Ugh! Waiting in the park across the street would've been a better choice, but since the girl had left already, she wouldn't know where to find me. One lump skittered along the edge of the shadows, cut a hairpin turn at my foot, and vanished beneath the bed. Normally this would have been the last straw to send me bolting out the door, but where was there to go? I sighed, closed my eyes, and gave in to my weariness.

Voices outside the door woke me. The sound of men talking Spanish came closer. I got my legs uncramped enough to stand, and did deep knee bends to limber up and start circulation to my numb feet. Who would've believed you could actually sleep in such a position? After a commotion outside, Bernardo burst in the door. His face lit up with a smile that exposed missing teeth. "Niño del Desierto!"

I hadn't heard that name since my first trip to Mexico. Shaking my drowsiness off, I sprang across the room into Bernardo's arms.

"Justin!" Victor exclaimed, never having learned my right name, but who cared? Unlike his friend, he didn't quite squeeze all the air out of my lungs.

As usual, none of us could communicate beyond handshakes, nods, and pats on the back. Afterward, I looked past the two men and noticed with some disappointment that the flat-faced girl hadn't returned, although her absence at least solved the problem of having to break a hundred to pay her, or so I thought. A kid, younger than me, stepped out from behind the two men. Something told me he'd come in her place.

Baby-faced, with round, chocolate eyes, he stuck his hand out. Misinterpreting his motive, I moved to shake his hand when the palm turned up. The fingers flexed in the universal sign for "Gimme." My heart sank. So then, the problem of breaking a hundred-dollar bill hadn't been solved after all. I had a feeling I'd just met the messenger. "Did the girl send you?"

"Si. Rosa."

Oh, great! Another non-English speaker. But at least I'd learned the girl's name. "Did Rosa send'um you'um to get'um Bernardo and Victor?"

"Who are we?" he asked with barely an accent. "Tonto and the Lone Ranger?"

"Oh, so you speak English."

"Why not? I went to school in Del Rio. I lived right across the border in Acuna with my grandma. I spent most my time on the American side."

"Really? But how'd you get word to San Miguel and back so fast, especially at night? It took us all day in Victor's truck."

"*Caballo*—a horse," he said, intending to teach me Spanish it seemed. "I borrow." He smiled in a way that made me wonder if the owner had been a party to the loan. "No roads to San Miguel. The trip much faster across country."

"Smart. No flat tires or breakdowns either." Behind the kid, through the partially opened door, an edge of sky revealed a purplish predawn light. I must've slept all night. No wonder my legs knotted. Not only that, but it also indicated Bernardo and Victor hadn't slept. The drive here in the dark with only headlights to see by must have been nothing short of a roller-coaster ride.

"You pay now," the kid said. All this time he had his hand out. "Fifteen."

"*Fifteen*? Your sister told me five."

"She tell me fifteen."

I seriously doubted that, but then again nothing had been in writing. Besides, the debt couldn't be paid whatever the amount, so my only option was delay. "We'll wait for the girl then. When she comes, she'll tell us."

"She not come." A look came over his face I didn't quite understand. "No?"

"After we leave, maybe. Then come."

I understood now. Those of us who make bad choices in life aren't crazy about being around family. "So, what's your name?"

"Raul," he chirped, his eyes shining. "Everyone know Raul. You want job done, call Raul. Want errand run, call Raul. He work *muy rapido*—very fast, but for price."

I pondered that. Raul, huh? Something warned me to keep a watch on Raul. The way his feet shifted around, hardly ever staying in one spot, with his eyes roving all over, rarely looking directly at me, made me uneasy.

"You pay now," Raul said, all this time with his hand out.

Before I could explain, Victor's huge form jumped between us and slapped the hand away, rattling in Spanish at Raul. The man's angry glare along with his raised volume had all the earmarks of a scolding. The two argued, but then Bernardo joined in, and Raul, with big pouty eyes, looked off.

"Mi tio say no," he grumbled. "Say you family. I can't charge. It not fair, but they the boss, for now. But you owe me."

"I'll pay, don't worry." Although relieved at not having to explain my money problems, I nevertheless saw Raul as essential, mainly because of his ability to speak English. It didn't make sense to lose his help over a misunderstanding. "But later, not right now."

His face brightened. "Good," he said, returning to his former restless self. "I'm very good amigo—*friend*—to have around. Very fast."

"I'm sure. I need you to translate for me with Bernardo and Victor, okay?"

His face fell. Because of his boyish looks, his feelings could be read like a book. "I no like translating. *Muy dificil*—very difficult. Hard to find right words with same meaning."

"I'll pay for that, too." As I suspected, he cheered right up. With him, evidently everything had its price. As Bernardo and Victor discussed something, I dug in my pocket and found a quarter, slipping it to him.

He grinned and pocketed the coin.

I then told Bernardo and Victor, with Raul interpreting, of how after leaving the two men on the banks of the Rio Grande on my first trip to Mexico, I'd been picked up hitchhiking by the cowboy-turned-thief outside El Paso, of surrendering to the highway patrolman, of finding out there'd been no crime like I feared, and, finally, of the man in the burning shack actually being a dummy. Raul ended up right, after all. Some words just don't translate. No one, even Raul, could understand what I meant by "dummy" or "plastic people" or "mannequin." By the end of my story, though, the men had a hearty laugh, indicating they understood me to be innocent of any crime.

Next, I told the two men the reason for my return to Mexico: that my friend was out in the desert at some kind of "camp," or whatever, that I had to go out and find the place because he might be in trouble and need my help. Midway through my story, at the word "camp," both their faces fell. Then, whispering in tones that needed no translation to tell me something alarmed them, they motioned for Raul to interpret. Greedy as ever, he held out his hand. Victor rapped him with a knuckle on the forehead.

"They say not good," Raul mumbled, rubbing the red spot below his hairline. "He say what out in desert is *muy malo*—very bad. Young men go out and no come back. His own son is here one day, gone the next. Never hear from again. Rumors say men gather in secret far away from others. That's why people in village no help him find mules you bring back. You stay away from this camp in the desert. Evil out there." He glanced at the two men; then leaned next to me. "They scared old cows. Not me."

I should've expected as much. Everyone so far had been against the idea. "Tell them they don't understand. He's my friend, my best friend. Bernardo wouldn't abandon Victor out there, would he?" I turned from one man to the other. "No, of course not. I must go find him."

Hearing his name evidently, Victor chimed as well. Raul interpreted. "He say you must listen, Justin. Why he call you Justin?"

I waved him off. "It's a long story."

"Oh. Anyway, he say men in desert are danger. Take young boys. They steal from towns, off farms, on streets. In desert is *problema grande*—big problem." Raul rolled his eyes dismissively.

Their warnings actually gave me pause. Who should I trust? Raul? Or the two men? Had the old guys exaggerated? After all, everyone knows how simple country people are prone to superstition. Before I could answer, Victor started in again. Raul interpreted.

"He say go home and forget your friend. You too small for this. Army cannot stop these *hombres malo*—bad men. How can you?"

That might have ended it except I had one more ace in the hole to play. "Tell them two-hundred dollars. Whoever acts as my guide gets two hundred in cash."

Raul didn't translate at first. Instead, he stared at me like he was seeing me for the first time.

I motioned for him to go ahead. "Tell them two-hundred dollars cash money. I know most of the way to the camp already." A little over optimistic on my part, but how else could I convince them? "All we have to do is follow a clearly marked trail made by these giant tire prints." Assuming, of course, we found them.

If we'd been in a card game, Raul just lost his poker face. He beamed a royal flush grin and jabbered in Spanish to the two men, but I could tell from their looks it didn't go right. Sure enough, Bernardo rolled his head and his smile dropped away.

Raul's recent delight turned downcast. "Bernardo say why you make him sad? He say him and Victor so glad to see you but you hurt their hearts. They no want money. Americans think only money. He say, 'Bah! Time to go home.'" Raul put a hand to the side of his mouth. "That them, not me."

"Okay, okay." I stopped both men from leaving. "I'm sorry. Tell them I'm sorry, Raul. It's just that I'm worried about my friend. He's in trouble, but I won't mention money anymore, cross my heart. Ask them to stay, please."

Raul translated and the old man nodded, but judging from Bernardo's tired look, he relented more out of exhaustion than anything. Raul, on the other hand, started acting weird. He dusted off my shoulders, asked if I wanted something to eat or drink, asked if I'd be more comfortable at his place, and generally reminded me of one of those tray-carrying street vendors the first time I'd crossed the border. As I recalled, those vendors turned mean after not getting what they wanted.

Then again, maybe I'd misjudged Raul as he began acting just as attentive to the two old men as he did me, insisting they rest while he drove

Victor's pickup across town to his place for blankets and pillows. No one made a move toward the bed.

When Raul came back, I offered to stay awake because of the rats, but to tell the truth, no one seemed overly concerned about them. I couldn't sleep anyway, not only because of just waking up, but worries about Hect made me restless. How would I ever find him now? Without a guide who knew Juarez, I couldn't even locate the road out of the city, much less the way to the camp. Should I go back home then? But how could I give up? What kind of person abandons his best friend? A jerk, that's who.

I felt a pull on one pant leg. Raul's baby face grinned up at me from my feet. He crooked a finger in a follow-me motion. The gleam in his eyes told me all I needed to know. I started to go for my travel bag, but after thinking about it, I decided that even though the two men snored peacefully, it'd be too risky. While crawling on all fours toward the front door, I paused beside Bernardo's sleeping form. After quietly removing my shoe and sock, I peeled two one-hundred dollar bills from my nest egg and, on second thought, added a third; then ever so gently slid them into the man's front shirt pocket. If nothing else went right from here on, at least I'd paid him back for feeding and housing me after I came out of the desert on my first trip to Juarez. Hopefully this was enough to save his farm from creditors.

Raul crept out the front with me close behind. After easing the door closed, we fled down a dark street. Neither of us spoke till we reached Victor's multicolored pickup.

"I drive." Raul held out a set of keys.

So that's why he'd been so eager to help and get the pillows and blankets. I hadn't misjudged the little sneak after all.

"Old goats very weak, very tired. We leave them behind." He giggled, confirming my impression that I shouldn't fall for his sweet, baby-faced looks. "No wake up."

He started the truck and shifted into gear like an expert, which considering his young age, surprised me. As we started down the dark street, I felt what was coming before he said anything.

"You pay two hundred now. Add fifty more."

I had already prepared an answer. "A deal's a deal. Two, no more." Actually, if he had pushed me, I might've given in, but a bluff seemed worth a try. "Drive me first, then get paid."

"Let me see."

Despite warning alarms going off inside, I removed my shoe and, while partially dragging down my sock, flipped through the hundred-dollar bills. It struck me how fast money went. The first hundred had vanished before I ever got to Mexico, then three more to Bernardo, now two to Raul; that only left four to get Hect and me back home. I didn't regret spending any of it, but just the same, I'd have to watch every penny from here on.

Raul stopped the truck. "You pay now, or go back."

"*What?*"

"Pay now."

I studied Raul. Was he bluffing? Judging by his feverish look, he knew he had me. Besides that, what other choice did I have? He might be faking, but he might not. "Okay." I peeled off a couple of hundred-dollar bills and tore them in half, bringing a gasp from Raul; then I gave him two halves. "You get the others once we get there."

Raul held up the pieces, turning them this way and that, but no matter how hard he tried to fit the edges together, they wouldn't match. All the same, he acted as if he held a fortune and stuffed the pieces in his shirt pocket. The pickup accelerated.

"Go to the Juarez jail first." I didn't have the nerve to tell him about the desert yet. Not all at once. A step at a time.

"*Cárcel!*" He stopped again and looked stricken. "Jail?"

"Just to begin. I'll show you where to go after that. Once I recognize the street, it'll be a snap which direction to take." At least I hoped so.

"Yes, yes." He started again. "Must be back before old roosters wake up."

I didn't have the heart to tell him we wouldn't make it in time. Anyway, who's to say we wouldn't? If the two men slept long enough, anything's possible, right? After all, how could I know how far into the desert the camp might be? From where I'd fallen off the truck, the place could be over the next rise. If so, we might make it back. Doubtful, very doubtful, but if Hect was ever to be rescued, worth a try.

We sped through dark streets, for once empty of the bumper-to-bumper smoking taxis. At the Juarez jail, everything looked the same, except that a wooden fence with rolls of barbed wire on top had replaced the electrified chicken wire. Also, steel beams had been planted around the perimeter, leaning outward, so that anything short of a Sherman tank would end up impaled. Fortunately, the highway that had taken Hect, Ju, and me out of the city was paved, unlike any of the other streets. "This is the road. Turn left."

"Left?" Raul asked, sounding taken aback. "That go to Chihuahua. Nothing out there. Only sand."

"We'll turn off and take another road." Still playing coy, I felt my time running out.

"Only empty nothing out there. Where to? You tell me now."

How could I not? We'd left the city behind. Besides, he'd know soon enough. "The desert." I pointed in the general direction of the rising sun.

"*Es muy grande*—very big! Where?"

"I'm not sure. To find a pair of big tire tracks. We'll follow them."

"Ay-yai-yai, big trouble. We no make it back before old men wake up. Two hundred not enough."

"Don't worry about Bernardo. He won't be mad. I left him money, lots of it, as much as he'll earn in a year. When we get back with my friend, I'll give them more. Victor, too. Money is no problem."

He snorted. "*No es problema*, eh?"

Despite an uneasy stirring, I felt he needed a push. "Okay, two-fifty, how's that?"

He smirked. Despite my having won round one, something told me that would not be the end of it.

CHAPTER 5
On the Trail

~~~

AN ORANGE CLOUD HID A rising sun above a gold-edged mountain range. Rather than admire the view, I recoiled at the sight. Sunrise to me would forever be connected with that morning in the desert on my first trip to Mexico when the start of a new day meant a long, drawn-out death under a cruel sun.

After leaving the city limits of Juarez far behind, I got curious about Raul. Who was he? What kind of guy had I thrown in with? He'd swiped a truck and disobeyed his uncle's orders not to go into the desert, knowing he'd get in big trouble, and all for cash, but who could blame him for being money hungry in these claw-to-survive surroundings? He also had a trickster's heart, offering to get blankets when he really wanted the truck keys and, while respectful when face-to-face with Bernardo and Victor, behind their backs he ran them down. But more disturbing than any of that, he seemed to have no feelings for his own flesh-and-blood sister. Was such a coldhearted person dependable? Could I trust him? And yet, to look at his baby face, anyone would think he never had a bad thought. So then, did he have any loyalty about him at all? How else to find out, but to ask? "Hey Raul, your sister, what was her name again?"

"Rosa."

"Rosa, that's right. Where'd she go?" I could only see his profile, making it difficult to read his reactions. "Why didn't she come back?"

"Victor."

"How come?"

"Problema—trouble."

I thought I'd give Spanish a try. "Pra-blem…"

"No-no, prO-blem-a. PrO-blema."

"PrO-blema."

"Mejor—better." He glanced over and smiled, seeming pleased at my trying to learn.

"So, you'd rather not talk about it, I take it."

"She have *un niño*—kid."

"Knee-o?"

"No, no. **Neen**. Neen-yo. Niño."

"Niño."

"Si. The father hombre malo—bad man. Victor told her to stay away from him, so she ran off and marry. He leave. Now she stay away."

"Victor sounds like her dad, not her tio." I waited for a reaction, hoping he'd noticed I knew the Spanish word for uncle, but didn't get any.

"Papá dead. Victor now her papá. He'd forgive, but she no ask. She afraid *el holgazán*—the deadbeat—will come back and…"

He kept talking, but something distracted me. Even though this highway had to be the same one that Hect, Ju, and I took when we escaped from the Juarez jail, until I found that prison movie set that I'd seen on my first trip to Mexico, there'd be no way to be sure which road to take into the desert. The ride already seemed farther than that first time. Just as I worried we'd gone on a wild-goose chase, we rounded a curve, and there stood the abandoned movie set dungeon. Just like the first time I'd seen it, the place looked like somewhere Count Dracula might live.

Actually, I'd only seen the place at night, but in the morning light the abandoned movie set looked exactly as Hect described it. Out of the sand arose a stone cliff covered halfway up by ivy, fake of course, as nothing so green lived out here, with guard towers on either end. To get from the highway to the entrance, two heavy wooden gates had to be passed through, one at the road and one at a much-sturdier rock fence with a sentry booth. Huge poles in the middle anchored each gate, but gaps on either end showed none of the departing movie people bothered to chain and padlock the gates.

When I faced back around, it was almost too late. "Raul! This exit! Take it!"

At a highway Y, we took the right turnoff, then circled underneath the road and kept going until making a Q. I'd never forget that first turn from my initial trip. Having burned my hand on the exhaust pipe, I had been forced to hold on for dear life with my other one to keep from flying off the truck.

As we headed south, the pavement's condition worsened, causing us to reduce our speed. Not only that, but an occasional mule-drawn cart slowed us even more. We dead-ended into another road whose main difference from the surrounding desert were piles of rocks now and then.

"Go left." I knew the way because that night on the truck I'd been thrown over against Hect and I remembered how glad I'd been to have him as a barrier. Ju had been my backstop at the next turnoff. "When you come to a right, take it."

After the turns, we drove through an opening in a wire fence with a familiar rumble. At the cattle guard, I knew what came next. "Bump ahead—watch out!"

Raul tried to slow, but both our heads hit the roof anyway. Dust flew up around us as it had the night on the truck. We'd arrived in wide open desert. Our speed was reduced by the hard-baked sand, but I felt reasonably certain that, with more daylight, we'd find those tire prints.

The view stretched from one mountain range across a flat basin to another set of high peaks. I well remembered those distant foothills. One of them had tricked me into leaving the giant tire tracks to chase colored lights that vanished with a rising sun. As if the first trip were happening all over again, the same sickening terror gripped me. The awful dread lasted until we came across gigantic tire grooves in the sand. Considering all the suffering I'd gone through searching for those imprints, they looked disappointingly ordinary.

One thing became clear, though. Considering all the twists and turns and distance, I never had a hope of walking out of the desert. If those doves hadn't shown up to lead me to the windmill, not to mention the mules who took me to safety, the only thing left of me would've been scattered coyote-gnawed bones. I silently thanked God for the miracle and promised to start attending church once I got back home, *if* I got back home.

We drove on top of the tire tracks. The ruts, though rounded off by the wind and partially filled in, ran on in the sand, disappearing now and then at a ravine dug out by rare floods. Crossing them could be tricky because of the steep banks and all the debris that washed down from the mountains. Once on the other side, though, the trail picked up again. We stopped several times and got out, looking for my footprints, but nothing came of it.

"Esto no es bueno," Raul said at one such stop.

Something was wrong, obviously. "What is it?"

"*Caliente.*" He pointed through the steering wheel at the dash.

Sure enough, the needle on the temperature gauge had passed the halfway mark on its way to "H." The radiator might soon boil over, locking up the motor. I scanned the desert, trying to get oriented. "There!" I'd never forget those mountains. "Water."

He snorted. "Loco."

"I'm not crazy either." That word needed no translation. "A mile or so from here. Mile and a half maybe, there's water, I tell you."

"No es real."

"Not that silvery heat-lake mirage on the horizon, I'm talking actual wet water. There's a tank out there with a pond. I drank out of it less than a month ago. If we can only find a high enough rise, you'll see the windmill." I told him a shortened version of the story of Half-Ear and the other two mules rescuing me.

Judging by the frown on Raul's boyish face, he wasn't convinced, but what other choice did he have? We couldn't make it back to Juarez with the gauge needle already nudging "H."

To leave the tire prints for open desert brought up all kinds of anxious feelings from my previous experience being lost. Plus now I had Raul to worry about. What if I couldn't find the windmill? Or maybe the fan had stopped turning. Added to that, this time there'd be no mules to carry us to safety. Anything could go wrong.

Raul drove us to the highest ridge that overlooked the entire basin. A faraway speck caught my eye. "There!"

He didn't see it at first.

"Right there!" I took him by a sweaty arm and pointed. "See? It doesn't look like much, but there's water." Admittedly, the windmill looked far away. With the needle so close to "H," we might melt the engine halfway there and really end up in a jam.

Raul hit the accelerator and we barreled down the slope. Before long, a tower in the middle of a clump of brush stood out on the flat desert. At the sight of propellers turning, I couldn't resist bragging. "Didn't I tell you? I fixed that windmill by myself. With no tools."

We both war-whooped and yahooed. Not only did the trough turn out brimful, but the pond had reached its banks. No telling how many drowned scorpions lay under those brown waters, including my old enemy Blacky perhaps. Personally, I hoped every last one of them was there. Among the leafless limbs that once shaded me from a blistering sun the day before my rescue, green twigs had already sprouted.

With the engine still running, Raul splashed water on the radiator before taking the cap off to prevent a boiling eruption. Victor's coffee cup proved a slow but adequate method to refill the radiator. Afterward, we took turns soaking in the trough while we waited for the motor to cool, then headed back the way we came. As soon as we reached the giant tire tracks, he stopped the pickup. "Go home now."

"Home?" I tried not to overreact. "Now? After all this? But we're so close." Even though I didn't know that, it wasn't a complete lie. We had to be closer than when we started.

"Gas low. Engine hot again very soon."

"But we're almost there. We have to be."

He looked off the direction we'd come. If he turned the steering wheel and headed that way, there'd be no turning back. I had to think fast. "Another fifty."

He didn't react.

I hated to start bribing, but what else was there? "If you keep going, three hundred."

"No enough."

I had a sick feeling, but we both knew he had me. And yet, if I agreed too readily, what was to stop him from pressuring me for more? In a way, though, I couldn't blame him. Except that it meant abandoning my friend, I'd have turned back long ago. Before I could answer, he pointed. "There!"

"What?"

"Problema."

I saw what he meant. A brown funnel the size of a dust devil lifted off the desert floor, but the bottom moved so fast that the whirlwind lay over at a sharp angle. Only one thing could speed across open desert like that. Sure enough, the forward part of a jeep poked out of the trailing cloud. Not long afterward, the heads of two males could be seen through the front windshield. My heart pounded. Who could be way out here, and what did they want?

The jeep slid to a stop amid a mini-sandstorm that rolled over us. When the air thinned enough so that we could see, two young fellows, neither one smiling and both dressed alike in T-shirts and khakis, walked toward us. I instinctively made the first gesture, as my dad had taught me years ago, and extended my hand for a friendly shake.

An opposing hand came toward mine, then shot up, snaked around my neck, and trapped my head in a muscular arm. We fell together. His body landed on my chest as the air gushed from my lungs. I kept trying to shake hands, hoping to show him my harmless intent, but about then I caught a glimpse of a descending fist, followed by a squashy thud over my ear. A sharp pain filled my head; then blackness.

CHAPTER 6
Centipede

I DARED NOT MOVE A muscle. All around me angry cries and shouted commands, as well as a hurried rustling, could be heard. Because of the hectic activity, I knew better than to move. Before long, the commotion died down. At last the place grew quiet. And yet, despite trying, I couldn't wake up all the way. As if trapped in a half-sleep like being under some sort of icecap, I searched around for an air hole to the surface but, unable to find one, drifted back down into the murky darkness.

The next time I woke up, it still seemed too risky to open my eyes. My aching head hadn't cleared enough to figure things out. Had all this been a nightmare? Juarez? Raul? Crossing the desert? The thugs in the jeep? A sore spot above my ear, along with an ache radiating from the tender area cast doubt on the last part. With that, my attention all at once shifted to my foot, or rather to my foot inside my sock—*an otherwise empty sock.* My heart sank. Gone! I felt it. My nest egg—all of it! That brought home reality. Bad dreams aren't thieves.

Despite having been robbed, I still didn't move. Anyone could be watching. Even the thief. Ever so carefully, I stole a peek out one eye. No one was in sight, so I inched both eyelids apart. Still I saw only an empty room. It seemed safe enough to look up and down without moving my head.

A long rectangular building appeared vacant, at least the part I could see. Across from me, metal shelves lined the walls from floor to ceiling. The bunks were attached by hinges to the wall and secured with chains to the outer corners. All the beds had been made up neatly with covers tucked tight under thin mattresses and pillows arranged into perfect squares.

Hearing a groan, I shut my eyes again but just as quickly opened them. Having recognized the source, I rolled onto my back, slipped a foot from under the cover, and gave a shove to the tin shelf above.

"Ayeii! No mas!" Raul cried nasally. He kept on in Spanish, honking like he had his nose pinched closed. From his tone, it might've been better that I couldn't understand.

"Raul? Is that you?"

"Who you think, Pancho Villa?"

He'd awakened in a bad mood obviously. "Are you hurt?"

"Aye-ya-ya. Feel like million pesos."

I overlooked the sarcasm. "No, really, are you okay?"

He answered in Spanish.

"Speak English."

"My nose, they break it, but I fight back."

"Ouch. Anything else?"

"Beat me all over. Ache everywhere."

Even though I was glad to hear a familiar voice, I cringed inside, thinking what trouble I'd caused the poor kid. Not only had he been roughed up, but whatever we'd gotten into, judging by our reception, it couldn't be good. And whose fault was it? Mine, as usual. Everyone so far had warned me, but would I listen? No. Again, par for the course. Raul was due an apology, but I didn't know how to go about it and decided to ease my way into it. "Gee whiz, Raul. Looks like I've gotten us into a mess, and there's no telling where we are."

"Army."

With that one word, all sympathy vanished. "Are you nuts? What's the matter with you? That's your problem, you say the first dumb thing that comes to mind. Don't joke around like that. You scared me out of my wits. I thought you were ser—." Then it hit me. "You *are* serious!"

46

"Si."

"But I thought...I mean...*army!* What army? That can't be."

"Army, still."

"For Mexico?"

"Mexican army not steal people. Other army."

"Other?" That gave me a whole new perspective. "So this is a barracks?"

"Si. Army camp."

Everything made sense. *Camp!* Of course. That's what Ju had meant on the back of that truck. A camp. But what kind of camp? Not an army camp, surely. The idea was just too awful. There had to be another explanation. "Hold on, Raul, let's not jump to conclusions. There're other kinds of camps, there must be. So what if this is a barracks? Barracks are everywhere. We could be in...in...say, well, let's see, a...oh...a *mining* camp! Why not that?" The idea sounded a lot less harrowing. "That's it. A mining camp. That's why those two guards jumped us—protecting their claim. We'll have to convince them that we don't care about or want whatever minerals they're digging for."

Raul hung over the edge of the bunk, peering down. His red eyes sparkled amid bruises on either side of a purple nose. Blood crumbs crusted around his nostrils. "So they mining, you say?" he asked nasally. "What they mine for, you think?"

"Who knows? But from the commotion I heard this morning, it's a big crew."

"Sand? They mine sand?"

"No, not sand. Nobody wants sand. There's miles and miles of that."

"Hmm. Sandstone?"

"No, there's no value in that either. Something rare."

"Sand dollars?"

That gave me pause. Sarcasm? At a time like this? Surely not. His upside-down face didn't give a hint. Since his first language wasn't English, he might've chosen the wrong word. "No, those are on the beach."

"Sand castles?"

I searched his battered face. Could it be? Was it even possible? Somehow it just didn't fit for him to be mocking me. His earnest look remained unreadable. "No." I'd answered cautiously. "Not them either."

"Sand-wiches."

"All right, very funny. Really. You're a scream."

He chuckled and rolled onto his back.

"I hope you know this is no joking matter." Scolding him just made me feel all the more ridiculous. For him to make fun had been the last thing I'd expected. It showed a whole new side to Raul. He might be sharper than I thought. "Okay, forget mining."

"This morning while you sleep I talk to man with white eye. I ask him where we are. He say town of...town of...spirits?"

"You mean, ghost town?"

"Si, si. He told me we in army. He say there more camps like this one. He say we work very hard to get to next one. He say be very careful, though. Make no mistakes. He say *hombre muy malo*—very bad man—is *patron* here. El Ciempies."

"Who?"

"No say in *ingles*. Ciempies is ugly worm, many feet, very hard sting."

"Centipede?"

"Si. Cen-ti-pede, that it, but he call him El Ciempies. He say very mean hombre."

"I hate centipedes."

"Not too loud," Raul whispered. "Man with white eye tell me no one say that to his face. He have very bad temper, make life very hard here. He say Cen-ti-pede have joy in giving pain to others. Everyone afraid."

"That's double the reason to quit this army, whatever it is."

"Si."

"What're the chances of convincing them we just came to pick up my friend, that's all?"

"Give us go-away party, you think?"

Caught off guard a second time, I had to admit the tongue-in-cheek remark made sense. "Yeah, I suppose you're right. No chance."

"We in army now," Raul said. "Man with white eye, he say he no join too. He say his mama sell him so other kids have food. He say they come from all over—Mexico, Costa Rica, Guatemala, and now *Norteamericanos*. They like boys, he say, that no one look for. No one care about."

Despite the fact that the news practically knocked the air out of me, everything started adding up. "So, that's why Ju took us with him when he escaped the Juarez jail." The next realization hit hardest of all. "We've been shanghaied."

"No understand."

"Kidnapped."

"Oh, si."

"Like the French Foreign Legion in the movies—forced to join against our will."

"Si."

"It'd been kinder to kill us out in the desert. We'll never get out of here." At that moment the outlook couldn't have looked bleaker. What had I gotten us into? It seemed the worst fate imaginable.

"I think on this all morning while you sleep," Raul said. "If we tell them we no want to join and must leave, no trust us. Watch us everywhere we go. Not good. We must act like we glad to join, happy very much. Make them think we come out here on purpose to be in army. They trust us, maybe? Maybe, when they not look, we get chance to sneak away."

Not bad. Not bad at all. The longer I got to know Raul, the more I saw him as no dummy. "Good point, my friend. Excellent point. Otherwise, they'd be expecting us to try and get away."

"Si."

"So we'll act like we heard a rumor and came out into the desert to find this place so we could enlist. That's sure to earn us extra points. Meantime, we'll search for my friend." I'd gained a new respect for Raul, who seemed full of surprises. "Hey, while we're at it, maybe you can help me. You know that money in my sock? It's gone."

"Ay, caramba, too bad."

"They got my two-hundred halves as well. Did they get yours?"

"Si," he said, without taking time to look in his pockets.

His answer had an insincere ring about it, but I didn't say more. What would be the point? Anyone could have taken my money—the goons who beat us up, or else even someone in the barracks. It did strike me odd, though, that Raul, who'd lost his share of the money as well, took the news so calmly.

At a sound like boot heels drumming on a metal floor, I flattened out, doing my best to sink into the bunk and disappear. The rhythmic thump-thump-thump drew closer.

"Now then, lads," a man called, "you're missing a bonny day outside."

There was no mistaking that accent. Under different circumstances, I would have dropped my jaw. I'd know that voice anywhere. Still, who could believe it? The last time I'd heard that South African twang had been on the truck after our escape from the Juarez jail. After all this time, would he still be friendly? Had anything changed? Having no idea what to expect, I lay still.

"You're missing some jolly rollicking times, chaps." His half laugh removed the last doubt—it was Ju all right. "The other lads have long been out sporting. What a grand time they're having, too, clocking one another about with javelins, running, and generally roughhousing. You'll want to join the revelry tomorrow." The footsteps stopped at our bunks.

To keep on pretending sleep seemed silly, so I stirred as if just awakening, while at the same time throwing an arm over my nose and stealing a peek. Ju looked snappy in fatigues, glossy black boots laced up midway to the knee, and with ribbons on his chest. If there'd been any question we'd arrived in some type of military setting, the sight of the uniformed black man dispelled it. He stood ramrod straight.

"So, you're the lads they found in the desert," he said, evidently unaware of my identity. "Sorry about the rough stuff, but some of these

50

boys around here are a bit on the overzealous side. There's no need for it, actually."

I stirred, throwing the other arm over my face.

"Let me inform you chaps of some basic instructions. Today you may rest your injuries, but in the morning the routine will start. You'll rise before light and accompany the other fellows in their calisthenics and have a go at some physical activities." Here he gasped. *"Tim!"*

Discovered! There was no doubt in my mind that the jig was up. I lifted my arms off my face and cleared my throat. "Er, why...yes. It, um...it's me."

"My boy, I'm flabbergasted. Don't tell me that it's actually you."

"It is." I raised up on one elbow. "Yes, it's me."

"Well, bowl me cockeyed!" Ju's gaping face couldn't have looked more surprised. "Why, when I caught sight of that mug you could have knocked me down like ninepins. Where'd you come from, lad?"

"The desert."

"But I thought you'd been killed when you fell under the truck. How in the name of blazes did you manage to survive?"

"I came across a water hole."

He shook my hand heartily. "You can't mean you've been in the desert this whole time."

"Not the whole time." I thought about mentioning going back to Texas but decided to skip it. "My friend Raul brought me here."

"Blimey, so you're saying you came here on purpose?" From his tone, he found that hard to believe. "Why?"

What better time to enact Raul's idea, although, admittedly, it went against my grain. "We came to join up."

"You actually *want* to join?"

"Yes, we do."

"You don't say, but how'd you know about us?"

Thankfully, I'd already prepared for that. "If you remember, sir, you yourself told me. When we were on the back of the truck, you said we were headed to a camp. I just put two and two together, is all, and decided to come out this way and find you."

"Smashing! Tell me the rest of the story, lad. What's happened since last we met?"

"It's a pretty long story."

"The short version then."

"The short version is, after falling off the truck, I made it to a village and stayed there until recovered from the desert. Raul and I became friends, and he drove me out here. He wants to join as well."

"You don't say? But how'd you locate us?"

"The tire prints. We tracked them here."

"Bloody clever. I must remember to send someone out to erase them." He stepped back and appeared thoughtful. "So, the two of you want to join up, do you? And here I would have ventured to say you came looking for your chum, Hect."

"That's part of it." I had to think on the fly. "I figured he was here somewhere."

"No, he's moved up a camp, that one has. Your mate took to the routine around here like we drew it up especially for him. Never seen such a rabid trainee, as if he'd been looking for such structure all his life. The bloke's passed one level higher than anyone in his division and is quite the exemplary conscript, actually. But now, you've no idea what you're a part of, I take it?"

"No, not really."

"Well, well, how things have turned out. After the truck ran over you, I thought all you would be useful for was bayonet training." He laughed, but when Raul and I didn't join in, cleared his throat. "A bit of levity there, you see, as if your dead body would only be functional for targeting with long daggers."

I managed a half smile.

"Right-o," Ju sighed. "You know, it wouldn't hurt either of you to lighten up a measure, have a go at a chuckle now and then. It's no good to eat too much glum pie, if you get my drift. After all, our intent is not to kill you unless, that is, you eat what they serve at the mess hall." He roared but stopped abruptly. "Oh, leave it be then. I can see you're not in the mood. No doubt you're out of sorts after such a reception, but try and understand—we must remain on our guard around here. We have enemies, I'm sure you understand, who'd love to find out our locale."

Neither of us said anything.

"Enough of that. It's time you two learned the procedures here. From now on, you must address me as Commander and snap to attention in my presence. You will observe military formality from here on."

"Yes, sir." I couldn't help but think that I avoided military school for this.

"Si, Comandante," Raul spoke up.

"Now pay attention while I expound a brief history. Tim, I know when you, Hect, and I were incarcerated in Juarez, you weren't looking to join an organization such as this one, but I took the chance you'd adapt to it better than a Mexican prison, especially as those convict savages wanted your hide for a pin-up. Actually, I'm always on the spy for young chaps who can think beyond girls and rum. Once I select them, it's generally an inopportune time to fill in the details. We're forced to move fast and remain hush-hush about it. That's why, before I conscript a bloke, I make sure he has no place else to go. You two being on the run from the law, as you Yanks say, fit the bill perfectly. Now then, pop over to the mess hall, and you'll be shown a film on our organization. Think of it as orientation."

We each climbed down from our bunks. We both squared up our pants and tucked in our shirttails. Although uncertain how exactly to stand at attention, I tucked my chin, at the same time ignoring, as best I could, a throbbing above my right ear, and squared my shoulders. As we turned to leave, Ju halted us.

"No-no, lads. Protocol. Before making an exit, you order up."

I spun around and faced my bunk. "French toast with sausage, sir."

Ju laughed so hard he had to grab hold of the cot frame. "That's it! I knew with a little effort I'd get you blokes to lighten up. I say, Tim-lad, you're a bit of a card, too, I see. Oh, that's choice—I say 'order up' and you give me your breakfast wishes. I must remember that one."

During the exchange, Raul stood on my bed frame and smoothed the wrinkles out of his blanket, then pulled it tight and tucked the edges under his mattress. The bed ended up a neat rectangle. He next squared his pillow. I imitated his efforts the best I could. The results didn't look half-bad for a first try, if I did say so. We then followed the uniformed man down the hall, copying his erect stride while stealing sidelong, worried glances at each other.

CHAPTER 7

Camp Life

~⌒⟩

JU, OR RATHER FROM NOW on "Commander," I guessed, led us toward the last trailer in a line of four just like it. Behind that, a cook in an apron poured out a bucket of greasy liquid. Beyond him, a gray water tower had a sloppily painted death's-head above the word *Toxico*. The water tower stood out as prominent as a broken-down old ghost ship among all the deserted, collapsing structures. With the skull and crossbones over the empty town like a pirate's banner, the place couldn't have looked any spookier.

A man dressed in khakis and T-shirt came out of the last trailer and began to talk with the Commander. The T-shirted fellow's left eye had a gray spot or scar that covered the whole pupil. Because of the white eye, I knew that he must have been the one who Raul talked with this morning, the one who gave him the lowdown on our being in an army. He kept blinking and held his head turned slightly, instead of facing straight on, indicating the eye was blind. Raul elbowed me, confirming my suspicions it was him.

Behind the two men, a breeze toyed with a tumbleweed the size of a sports car. The ball of dried twigs rocked back and forth in the light wind, first moving a half roll this way, then next moving a half roll the other way, back and forth, unable to get out of its one spot. The bush reminded me of my own helplessness.

Ju and the other man continued talking as the T-shirted fellow winked the whole time like someone expecting a finger-poke in the eye. Once the two finished, I followed the Commander into the mess hall while Raul went the other direction. At the time, I thought little of our parting beyond a twinge of regret at the loss of company. No one likes facing troubles alone. It never crossed my mind that'd be the last time I ever saw Raul.

The room inside the long trailer felt stifling, offering no relief from the heat. Four tiny windows allowed practically no circulation. Rows of empty picnic tables stretched from front to back. Ju, or Commander, motioned me to sit facing the raised platform. A film began to play on a projector screen hanging from eyehooks in the ceiling.

A bearded man wearing a turban mumbled under the louder English voice of the translator. Because of the poor scratchy sound, along with a murmuring of whatever the original language had been, I leaned forward and cupped an ear.

"Most worthy emigrants," the voice said, broken up by heavy static, "each of you has been rescued from desperate circumstances—slums, border town ghettos, jails, and so forth. Many are from Latin cultures or else European, although recently recruits from the United States are join-ing our movement. Wherever you're from, your society has rejected you. To your family, if you ever had one, you are a burden they can no longer afford to keep. You are outcasts doomed to claw out a meager existence, hungry and diseased, left on the streets or in rat-infested prisons. You had no hope—no hope, that is, until we had pity and selected you. Why, you ask, did we bother? Why take you in, house you, clothe you, feed you, train you, and, most of all, give you a future? For one reason only, you were deemed capable of profiting us. You will from this point on serve our every dictate. Consider yourselves our property."

The voice droned on, but a fly landed on the table, distracting me. I watched it rub its front legs and comb the hair on its tiny head forward. One clap of my hands an inch or two above its flight path and that'd be the messy end. I'd killed no telling how many for my mother, who hated the pests worse than anything.

Speaking of mother, had she gotten my letter by now? And how had she taken the news? One thing, I bet my father was home. Would they un-derstand? Or be mad? Let's see, a school semester blown, a year's tuition lost, my half of the insurance settlement gone—no, not mad. Furious, maybe. Or, more likely, enraged. I could hear the yelling now—"You put us through all this to rescue that friend of yours, that school dropout, with no family to speak of, who we never approved of in the first place!"

Come to think of it, how would I ever find Hect now? If, as the Commander said, he had been promoted to another camp, I would only be able to catch up to him by being promoted as well. If Hect had been such an "exemplary recruit," then I'd have to be one better.

At that, I cast a sidelong glance in the direction of the Commander, who scowled back at me from a nearby table. With a disapproving frown, he pointed toward the film. I sat up quickly and leaned forward, chin in hand, hoping to imitate concentration, while at the same time quietly scolding myself for starting off with a poor first impression. From here on, that would be the end of daydreaming. I'd be a model pupil. If Hect had adapted and gotten promoted in record time, I'd do it even faster.

"Each one of you," the translator was saying, "will very soon be transformed from society's cast-offs into positions of professionalism. This rags-to-respectability alteration will occur in three phases. First, as trainees, you are to be selected and processed into the specialized fields we've chosen, mainly in the legal realm. Next, as apprentices, you will be thoroughly schooled. Third, you will become our representatives to be placed into predetermined locales in various societies. Once satisfied that you are fully qualified, we will equip you with official degrees representing the best universities, plus awards and credentials that will appear more authentic than originals. You will think, talk, and act as legal professionals ready to effect the cultural changes our leaders determine. Needless to say, you will carry out our directives to the letter, perfectly, flawlessly, or be suddenly removed, along with any family and connections you have formed. Don't doubt me on this. It will happen."

Despite my best intentions, the instructor's voice faded to a distant drone, much as it had in every classroom I'd ever attended. However, there were more pressing items that needed consideration. For one thing, how odd that circumstances worked out to land me in this place. Instead of military school, here I sat in this harshest of military camps. Was this revenge? Military school would've been a breeze. Was I caught up in a grand scheme to teach me "a lesson of a lifetime," as my mother had originally planned? Would the penalty ever end or go on forever?

A movement caught my eye. Over at the next table, the Commander motioned and jabbed a finger irritably toward the film. I sprang out of the slouch I'd slipped into and sat ramrod straight. If this kept up, instead of the top of my class, I'd be lucky to remain at the bottom.

"We are a unique society," the voice on the film went on, "whose dedication is to the abolishment of injustice in the form of nationalism, racism, and religion. Concerning nationalism, our struggle is for a world without borders; regarding racism, we embrace every ethnic origin and nationality and oppose only individualism; as far as religion, all faiths must combine into one common, encompassing deity conforming to our parameters of divinity. The only standard of conduct allowed in our society will be that which is best for those in harmony with us."

From then on, the Commander's stare never left. I used every schoolroom trick in the book to appear alert, from drumming my fingers on my chin to faking coughing spells to yawning with my mouth shut tight to biting my lip until my eyes watered. All in all, I made it to the end but even so, learned next to nothing. The screen went blank. I flinched and blinked away a stare.

"Well, lad," the Commander said, standing and approaching my table. "You've listened to some remarks from one of our leaders. I assume you paid close attention." His almond eyes narrowed.

I'd seen that same look from practically every teacher I'd ever had and, as a result, was hardly knocked off my stride. I smiled and nodded.

"In that case, you heard some bloody harsh criticisms directed at your homeland. Such censure ought to inspire a rebuttal on your part. So, speak up. Come on. Don't be alarmed. You can talk freely. Upon my word, there'll be no repercussions. If it's in your mind to show a bit of nationalistic pride for the land of your forefathers, have a go at it. This is your chance to clear the air. Let's hash it out and debate our differences."

I had no idea what he meant, but his tone had all the ear markings of a pop quiz. This was nothing new. Teachers had been trying to catch me not listening from the first day I'd been in school. Consequently, I looked thoughtful, but then shrugged.

"Come now, chap. All that criticism surely disrupted your convictions. Tell me some of them. In school you must have been taught worthwhile attributes of America, so let's hear about it. Stand your ground."

I tapped my chin, hoping to appear in the deepest contemplation, but then threw up my hands as if unable to think of one.

"Oh, blimey, lad. Those disparaging remarks you just heard most certainly made you gnash your molars. Tim-lad, you can't let the good old US of A be trounced on like that. Out with your defense. You surely learned something positive about your homeland somewhere along the line— its history, its form of government, its economic model, its character, its moral convictions, something!"

"Nothing, sir." I meant it, too. Even if I had been listening, nothing came to mind. Something should, perhaps. America had always been a good enough place to live, but then everyone else must feel the same about their country. What gave me the right to think mine any more special?

"Not one thing, is it?" the Commander said, sounding pleased. "You can't come up with even a single merit. To give you my honest opinion, I don't believe you give a fiddle about the land you left behind." After giving me that wide smile of his, we shook hands. "Tush, tush, old chap, congrats! You're the exact chap we hunt for."

Relieved to escape further grilling, I nevertheless felt crummy. It would have been nice to come up with at least some kind of defense. Actually, all I could think of was that we had elections, could vote, and had freedom, nothing else.

The sound of footfalls off a multitude approaching from outside the building cut me short.

"Sounds like marching, what? Why, bless my soul, your fellow recruits have completed their morning exercise so soon and are returning. The boys have developed quite an appetite, no doubt. Get ready, lad, you're about to meet your fellow recruits."

CHAPTER 8
A Hundred Sit-Ups

THAT PRETTY WELL ANSWERED MY question how I got into such a mess, but *not* how I would ever do a hundred sit-ups. All the time I'd been reminiscing about being at home, about my trip to Juarez and here, and about camp life so far, I'd been practicing sit-ups, but had never gotten above twenty. So how would I ever complete Centipede's number? Here I'd been lying in the same spot beneath a broiling sun for one unending afternoon, and after that, for an even longer freezing night. With sunrise fast approaching, if the desert floor beneath me turned into a lake, I'd drink it dry, or at least try. Breathing was agony because each gasp rasped my throat like I was sucking down sandpaper. The only thing crazier than the idea of me lasting one more day and night in the open like this was the notion of my doing a hundred sit-ups. There had to be another way. If only Centipede could be convinced that I finished without actually doing them. Maybe he'd believe me if I swore on my word of honor? Yeah, fat chance of that. I started doing sit-ups once more, this time making it to the incredible number of twenty-seven before collapsing.

Whenever I was tempted to quit trying, the prospect of staying in the open another twenty-four hours spurred me on. During rest breaks, my thoughts centered on whatever might encourage me to keep going. In school, teachers taught that threats don't motivate, that fear won't inspire achievement, that only rewards get results. I wondered about that now as the idea of disappointing Centipede had turned me into a bona fide workaholic. I cared less for sleep, for eating, even for water, despite being so thirsty, compared to doing just a couple more sit-ups. At one point, I achieved the unheard of number of thirty-two, but a sting in my groin forced me to stop. The strained muscle promptly stiffened up and from then on, the area got so sore with each attempt that, if there'd ever been a chance of reaching a hundred, all hope just died. Instead of trying any longer, I had no choice but to lay quiet and think. Before long, an idea came to mind, which at first seemed laughable, but after giving it some thought, I decided what else was there?

In order for my idea to have a chance of working, I'd have to try something new. I needed a distraction along the lines of the hand puppet I'd used for a prop at the mess hall table. Another ventriloquist gimmick that I'd practiced but never really cared for was to put something in my mouth. Some pros I'd seen used an unlit cigarette for a prop or bit into an apple, but that wouldn't work here. What about a scrap of cloth like tearing off a piece of my shirt? No, that would muffle the words. How about a stick then? That's it! I felt around in the sand until finding one the size of a half-smoked cigar. Put between my teeth, it should serve two purposes. First, Centipede would assume I strained so hard the stick kept me from breaking my teeth. And second, anyone watching me would think I couldn't possibly pronounce words, but just to make sure, I'd throw in a bit of theatrics. If everything went right, there might be a chance—an outside one for sure, but a chance.

With the arrival of daylight, whole groups of stars vanished from the sky. While I waited for Centipede and the others to show up, butterflies stirred in my empty stomach, the same ones that always came before a live performance. During my Joke Shop days, we'd try out new routines in front of audiences made up of families and friends, which sometimes worked and sometimes didn't. No matter how often I went on stage, the time before always dragged by in misery. To make matters even worse, I hadn't practiced my ventriloquism. Could I still throw my voice? Would my lips move noticeably on the labial sounds of f, v, b, p, and m? Back in the old days, after untold hours of practice in front of a mirror, I didn't worry about such things. Now, though, I felt as uncertain as a first-timer. I put the stick between my teeth and clamped down.

A rising sun in a cloudless sky promised another day in a furnace. The sounds of yawning and groaning accompanied the arrival of the recruits, who then formed a square around me. I waited for the inevitable and, sure enough, at the end of my feet, a pair of knee-high moccasins showed up. A form bent down, shading me, as calloused fingers cupped my chin. A shaft of sunlight over Centipede's shoulder forced me to shut my eyes and dip my head.

"Look!" The lanky leader shouted loud enough for all to hear. "He prays!"

Scattered titters arose from among the onlookers.

"Or he's sad his sock's empty." He laughed.

Now I knew who stole my nest egg. How else could the thieving leader know? I silently apologized to Raul, wherever he might be, for suspecting him. And yet, though Centipede's comment had been meant as a slur, what he'd said made sense. God helped me before, why not now? I silently asked Jesus forgiveness for not praying since then and made a brief plea for help. Whether a miracle like the first one came or not, I made up my mind to begin a regular routine of prayer, which, if my plan failed, might not be for very much longer.

"All eyes front!" Centipede announced at the tops of his lungs. "This rich boy, I hear, makes puppets and brings laughter at meals. So then, for every sit-up the American fails at, the formation will do ten. If he completes twenty only, you will finish with eight hundred. After that, see how funny you think your clown is."

I wanted to explain about my muscle strain, but after that, how could I?

"One hundred sit-ups! Begin!"

I started slowly, purposely slurring my words as if the stick in my mouth was to blame, and adding a gasp in between each number, "Un. Oof! Ooh. Oof! Ree. Oof!"

My groin, after my long rest, didn't hurt as much at first, but with each curl, the twinge worsened. Unable to see Centipede's face for the sun, I felt his eyes on me. In lifting my upper torso, I tilted my head back slightly, making it easy for him to see my mouth, "Ive. Oof! Ix. Oof! Even. Oof! "

At the top of each curl, with my nose inches from my knees, I paused long enough to gather my nerve. The butterflies in my stomach fluttered wildly. With the lanky leader standing over me, I uncoiled on my way to lying flat on my back. While turning my head ever slightly so the stick blocked any view of the side of my mouth aimed at the ground, I let go a long, extra-loud wheeze that ended with, *"Centipede!"*

The moccasin feet shifted this way and that, turning one way and then the other, as if trying to locate where the voice had come from. I kept on struggling through sit-ups as if nothing happened. Once at the top of my curl, I called the next numbers, slurring as usual. "Leven. Oof! Welve. Oof! Erteen. Oof!"

On the way back down, I went through the same process as before and ended an extended exhale with an even louder: *"Centipede!"*

The moccasin boots spun around in the opposite direction from that first time and sped away as sand divots covered me. A sidelong glance showed the thin-skinned leader's back going into the assembly. My only hope was that he would not come back very soon. I rested while counting out loud, though at a much faster tempo.

"Wenty—wenty-ive—hirty-one—hirty-ix—orty."

The whole time I kept one eye trained on the spot where the overly sensitive leader had vanished among the other bodies. "orty-ive—orty-even—ifty."

A rustling in the formation alerted me. I prepared to start up again. The buckskin-clad leader shoved aside two recruits in the first line of bodies as I lifted my torso. Knee-length moccasins took up the same position as before.

"Ifty-ine. Oof! Ixty! Oof!"

Every sit-up now began with a burning pain. From there, the sting shot from my groin through my stomach into my chest. Each time the muscle felt as if it were tearing afresh. If I quit now, the other boys would still have almost four hundred to do, but at the same time, I couldn't go on. With each effort, I ground my teeth, growling on the way up and hollering at the top as if that'd be the last one. As I dropped back from the tuck, the situation called for desperate measures. Having made up my mind, I drew in a bracing breath and blew out a great gush, ending with, *"Centipede's headless!"*

The moccasins leaped straight up and sprinted in yet another direction. As soon as my back hit the sand, I restrained a whimper, instead counting even faster than before.

"Eventy—Eventy-ix—Eventy-ine."

If Centipede returned, I might possibly do a few more, but not many. The fatigue, along with the constant ache in my groin, wouldn't allow it. Not only that, but based on the time that'd passed since the bad-tempered leader left, I figured he'd be back soon. I had to hurry.

"Inety—inety-ree!"

A Good Samaritan in the assembly cleared his throat and a good thing, too, as I'd lost track of which direction Centipede had taken. Except for the warning, I would not have known the foul-tempered leader had circled around behind me. Hardly able to lift myself, I pushed off with my elbow on the side of my body away from his approach, twisting and grimacing. Sure enough, the pair of moccasins arrived next to my head.

"Inety-ix. Oof! Aaaghf! Grrrr! Inety-even."

I dropped back and gulped air in great gasps. Grabbing a last breath, I struggled through another. The next one took all my reserves as I screamed a final: "Inety-ine!"

My back hit the ground in a dust cloud. I prayed. One shoulder lifted, then the other; my stomach muscles tightened as a hot lightning bolt, or what felt like it, shot through my middle. I raised my torso, yelling my lungs out, but once off the ground, fell back. The next try resulted in failure also. A third effort didn't make it halfway. As I lay there, gathering my strength for a fourth try, I heard something. A murmur. It began low and got louder. What was it? A chant? Yes, a chant that spread and lifted until all around.

"Hundred! Hundred!" And it grew in volume. "HUNDRED! HUNDRED!"

"Ahhh-aha-ahaaa!" Centipede shrieked, ending the repeated phrase. "Half rations today! Everyone! One word more, and you'll stay out here tonight!"

During the tirade, I noticed the toes of the cranky leader's moccasins pointed at an angle facing the formation. Spitting the stick out of my mouth, I pushed off with the hand on the opposite side of my body from Centipede. It was all I needed. "One hundred!"

"HURRAH!" went up a great shout. "HURRAH!"

Since the assembly had witnessed the whole deception, I took their cheers not so much as approval of me, but that we'd all shared in putting one over on the bossy leader.

Centipede's furious squawks overcame the jubilation at last.

"Tonight, no sleep!" he bellowed, swinging haymakers at imaginary opponents all around him. "Recruits form up here! Tomorrow you will not be so happy!"

I, on the other hand, hoped to rest a minute, being too exhausted to pay attention, but no such luck. The gangly giant grabbed me by the shirt front, lifted me as easily as a bag of dirty laundry, and set me on my feet.

"You'll be too clever for your own good one day." Centipede flashed an ugly grin of pink gums above gapped, stained teeth. "Smart alecks don't last long here. And when you stumble, I'll be there waiting." He then shoved me toward the assembly.

A space opened up in line. My knees buckled several times, but helpful fellows on either side caught my arms. After the bad-tempered leader spewed his usual rants, we all marched into the mess hall. Once we ringed the tables and stood at attention, a dipper full of water arrived in front of me from somewhere. My hands shook until I couldn't hold the ladle, so a neighbor lifted the cup rim to my lips as I tilted back my head. Sipping at first, and then swallowing, I regained strength from the liquid, stabilizing my knees. The next dipper I managed to hold.

The meal consisted of sour-tasting leafy vegetables with chunks of gristly meat. All the bowls had been filled only halfway as per Centipede's threat of half rations. At one time, I would've spit out such garbage, but now I downed it like a favorite dish.

With food in my stomach and after staying awake all night, my body craved sleep. As a result, during the film lecture that followed the meal, I tried not to doze off, but the warmer and stuffier the room got, the harder it became. The next thing I knew, Centipede stood over me, yelling his small head off. He cursed me with every vile name imaginable, but none hurt more than calling me "coward" before everyone. By the time he finished, I couldn't look up.

After the program and before anyone left the mess hall, the big fellow sitting next to me, the one who'd been first to shun me when I asked for a pencil and paper, and who also had been the first won over by my hand puppet, leaned close and pressed against my shoulder. "Amigo?" he said gruffly but quietly.

I glanced over.

"No worry," he whispered. "Everyone coward sometime; him too." He nodded toward our moody leader. "He so scared of water, he no shower. Put him in over his head, he not so brave."

That night, true to Centipede's threat, we spent the entire long hours of darkness standing in formation. Some actually slept while standing, leaning against their neighbor, but not me. I rehearsed in my mind how to get even with Centipede. All to no purpose, of course, as everyone knows bullies never get their due, but at least the boiling anger kept me awake, my heart pounding ninety-to-nothing.

CHAPTER 9

The Death Challenge

~⌒~

THAT ONE SLEEPLESS NIGHT WENT by like a daydream compared to the next couple of weeks. Awake before sunrise, we ran in the desert, did calisthenics until breakfast, and spent the rest of the day in the mess hall watching filmed lectures. Evenings dragged by in a supervised study hall with lights out by ten o'clock. Frankly, by that time I couldn't wait to go to bed. Especially in the beginning as I often traded meals for naps. The only exception to the routine happened when our work fell short of the standards for the day set by Centipede, who would then keep us up twenty-four hours straight. Sore muscles and aching joints became the norm, and bumps, bruises, or sprains never answered for an excuse to quit, unless accompanied by broken bones or loss of consciousness. Generally speaking, camp life reminded me of all the discipline I'd missed growing up rolled into one.

Of the recruits I encountered, the majority came from Latin countries; some were from Europe and a small number from the United States. Everyone had to learn English to start since that was expected to one day be the "universal language," as one teacher phrased it. Not only that, but each trainee must display an aptitude for such things as case law and legal documents, which made up the bulk of our studies. Anyone who couldn't memorize what seemed to me like volumes washed out. These poor souls disappeared without a word. Raul was one of them. The rumor came around that Centipede tried to help him study with the punishment box. Situated away from the trailers, the fearsome container was four feet tall by two feet wide. A person inside could neither stand nor sit, but must stay bent over at the waist. After a day in the "Box," it was said that Raul came out gray in color, talking in a crazed manner, with blood trickling from his nose. They rushed him to Consejo hospital in Ojinaga, or at least that's how the official version went. Few that I talked to believed it.

During this time, I experienced a brand new sensation. At the mention of a name, in this case "Centipede," a sour gas bubble would rise into my throat threatening to burst. Every night, my last thoughts involved the small-headed bully—rehashing what insults, cruelties, or humiliations he'd inflicted on me and other recruits during that day, and the different forms of revenge I imagined. Once asleep, though, the tables turned on me. In reoccurring nightmares, my enemy chased me all over while I ran in slow motion.

Camp life had its occasional bright spots, though. One morning I awoke earlier than anyone else in the barracks to find something had changed. My body felt different. No more soreness, no more stiffness. I swung my legs off the shelf and leaped from my middle bunk to the floor, landing catlike. In the only mirror around, on the back of the shower-room door, my reflection all but took my breath away. Overnight, or so it seemed, my body went from skinny to strapping, from droopy to hard. I had actual, defined, firm muscles, the physique I'd always dreamed of having.

If I'd been alone somewhere and not at a place where hollering at the top of my lungs would result in a hangman's party, I'd have let loose the biggest "Yaa-hoo!" ever. As it was, I had to be content with quietly striking weightlifter poses, knotting my biceps to the max, and bunching different muscle groups.

However, not for long as a sound outside the trailer soured my party. Centipede's high-pitched voice meant he would soon shriek that nerve-shattering reveille of his. At his cry, as irritating as fingernails on a chalkboard, everyone would bolt out of bed and form up outside the barracks to begin a day like any other. The thought sank my spirits even lower. The only part of my life not improving involved the bad-tempered leader. For whatever reasons, Centipede started off not liking me, and no matter how hard I tried or how patiently I endured his abuse, he simply would not be won over.

After the morning run and calisthenics, all of us recruits ended up standing in the mess hall waiting for Centipede's foul mood to improve. He often kept us at attention as our soup skimmed over or our hash grew cold, waiting on whoever would make the first restless twitch. Any adjustment, such as shifting a foot, or fidgeting, or stirring in any way, and the offender would be driven from the building, along with slaps, kicks, and curses, to work the rest the day digging a new latrine or whatever.

This time no one squirmed as we were allowed to sit down at long last. During the meal, Centipede made sure no one ate in peace as he railed about how we did this or that wrong or else how we should've done better at one thing or another. To tell the truth, I had other things on my mind as the boys at my table looked hangdog. Anyone could see they needed cheering up. After my discovery this morning in the shower-room mirror, I wanted to celebrate, not sit around having the blues. Besides, a hardy laugh would do everyone a world of good, and it wouldn't be an empty boast to say that I'd become the "headliner" at our table. After my first day at camp, when I did the hand-puppet trick to get a pencil and paper, I'd been doing gags and impersonations all along to entertain the guys. They'd come to expect it. This time then, inspired by our out-of-sorts leader ranting away up front, I impersonated Centipede with my hand puppet, goose-stepping around and acting the blowhard, but unlike other times, my audience didn't join in. They mostly stole nervous glances toward the front. What was needed was a new routine, something different, a real winner that'd overcome the comedian's curse. My only hope was fresh material, but what?

Just as things looked bleakest, an inspiration dawned. It couldn't have been any timelier if the cavalry arrived at the last moment. I happened to spot on my plate among the mixed vegetables a novelty—a string bean, a most unusual string bean. The stem split in the middle, branching into separate pods that looked remarkably like two legs. After selecting a pea from the pile on my plate and carefully balancing it on top of the pod, the veggie took on human form. By carefully, ever so carefully, rolling the bean between my thumb and forefinger, I made the figure appear to walk. The pea-head kept falling off, but this only added to the fun. I laughed as hard as anyone, despite knowing that a comedian should always maintain a straight face.

The redheaded recruit across from me, the same one who had a habit of butting in whenever I got rolling, leaned in and motioned everyone to gather in close. Hardly able to restrain a case of the giggles, he pointed at my figurine. "El Ciempies!"

Talk about coincidences. Red called it again. The figure *did* resemble Centipede, now more than ever because the unstable pea rolling everywhere was the spitting image of the leader "yelling his small head off." The table descended into suppressed hysterics. Some lay atop the table, others hid behind neighbors' backs, and still others collapsed on nearby shoulders, but all in all, my routine was the biggest triumph yet.

For the life of me, I couldn't help joining the laughter. I tried to act as if unable to understand what was so funny, but there was no help for it. The tears streamed down my cheeks and I sputtered uncontrollably every time the pea toppled off and rolled over the table. It became a game of who could catch Centipede's "head." In our fun, we lost all caution, especially as so many zingers came to mind that I couldn't whisper them fast enough. "Oops! I shouted my head off!"

Everyone grabbed for the pea bounding atop the table.

"Oh, no! You mashed it! Here, I've another! A hundred sit-ups!"

This brought down the house. More recruits from other tables gathered around.

I bent the headless string bean double as if doing sit-ups. "Ninety-nine! One hun—!"

Out of nowhere, a hand crashed down on the table, crushing my bean-pod, smashing veggie gore all over my fingers. My audience scattered.

An overly small face with paper-cut eyes leaned down. I drew back and raised my free arm in anticipation of a smack, but surprisingly none came. Instead, Centipede lifted his hand, freeing mine, and leaving behind a green mush pile. He then drove one fist into the other palm, ground it fiercely like a pestle in a mortar, and then flicked his thumb off his chin. Without so much as a word, he wheeled about and walked out of the mess hall, followed by the roomful in a scrambling herd. The scene left me bewildered. Whatever the leader meant by his gesture, it must have been important as no one finished his meal.

As the last recruit left the hall, I became aware of someone directly behind.

"Your theatrics were most clever, Texan."

I turned around to find a young man. Older than me, perhaps as much as in his twenties, I recognized him because of his white eye. He'd been the one who stopped to talk to Ju, or rather the Commander, on our way to the mess hall that first day. As before, he blinked the hurt eye constantly, but I was glad for his compliment. "Why, thanks."

"How'd you do that? I watched your mouth carefully. Not only did your lips not move, but the words sounded as if coming from the little puppet."

"Practice."

"I would like to learn how."

"Want another demonstration?"

"We don't have time, sad to say."

He had his head turned slightly, his good eye aimed at me. I felt tempted to lean over until face-to-face, but resisted the urge. "You called me 'Texan.' How'd you know?"

"I know lots about you, more than you'd ever guess. At the moment, though, I must have a word with you. You're a recent convert to our camp life, I know, so you don't understand the ways here."

"Why'd everyone leave?"

"A fight."

"That figures." I sighed. "The age-old attraction of watching some brute pound a weaker opponent senseless. Big deal. I think I'll remain here, thank you, and finish my dinner."

"But they are waiting for you."

"Let them wait. Personally, I prefer a good sunset."

"But they won't start without you."

"Oh, they'll start all right. You're mistaken there, my friend, believe me. A mob full of blood-lust care only to see suffering—someone else's, of course. They'll start the fight and never miss us."

"No, Texan, you're the one mistaken. They won't miss me. It's you they'll miss."

"How's that?"

"You're in the fight."

He might as well have karate chopped my throat. Unable to swallow, I could hardly get anything out. "Who?" I forced a dry gulp. *"Me?"*

"The one you so skillfully ridiculed, he's waiting for you."

I felt faint. *"Centipede?"* The room spun and I put a hand atop the table, trying to stop it. Nothing made sense. "B-But why?"

"You offended him."

"For impersonating him, you mean? It was only a joke, surely he knows that. He must. I was just having a little fun."

"No one has fun at this camp, certainly not at Centipede's expense."

The initial shock began to wear off and my mind cleared somewhat. "In America comedians mock people all the time and no one does anything about it, certainly not start fights. Otherwise, comics would stop insulting people." A waste of breath, obviously. My only hope seemed to be to take a different tack. "Okay, okay, I understand now. I hurt his feelings. I see that. All right, I'll walk out there right this minute and apologize."

"He will not accept your apology. In his mind, you have disgraced his authority in front of the entire camp. The only way for him to regain his position is to end your life."

"End...? *Kill me?*

"It's a pity, but yes."

"But, kill! Not kill! You're talking murder! That's against the law. Surely a joke is not worth going to jail over."

"Here it is not against the law. It is the way of our camp. Anyone can challenge anybody, as Centipede just did you. That was the motion he did with his hands. Such competitions to the death were once common in America. Duels they called them. Men used pistols and the best shot won, or the luckiest. They settled arguments and resolved disputes quickly, but here we are more civilized. Under our rules, the challenger must grant his opponent a choice, either of weapons or else fight locations. In your case, for example, should you decide not to select fighting tools, you must then pick the site of the contest."

"Does the Commander know about this?"

"Unfortunately, he cannot intervene. A challenge is sacred and cannot be withdrawn."

"But I won't do it. I'll refuse. They can't make me fight."

"In that case, you will die most savagely. Cowards are despised as much as the disloyal. On the other hand, a brave combatant is admired, and his end will be mercifully swift. Your only choice now is to pick the weapon you two will fight with or else where the battle will occur."

"B-B-But..." I regretted stammering but couldn't help it. "I-I'm not familiar with weapons."

The man rolled his head. "This is most unfortunate because your opponent is an expert. Not only is he skilled in killing instruments, but he is very strong and quick also. He specializes in guns and knives, but his bare hands are his most lethal devices. I think you better think hard and find what you are good at in the next few seconds."

The room surrounding me blurred. What a ridiculous idea that I would be good at any sort of fighting tools. My mother wouldn't even buy a toy pistol for a Christmas gift for fear the cap might burn my hand. My only talent had been ventriloquism and what good would that do? I thought of making a run for it, but where to go in this vast desert? Just as things seemed beyond hopeless, something outside the window caught my eye. A gray, metal ball hovered outside the mess hall as big as a flying saucer. The skull and crossbones painted sloppily on the side had me transfixed. How timely to see such an omen at a time like this—a death's-head.

CHAPTER 10

The Water Tower

~

WHILE HOLDING ONTO THE ARM of my new, half-blind friend, I made it across the mess hall on knees so shaky we might as well have been in an earthquake. Outside the trailer, we stood under an overhang on a patio barely big enough for two. Down at the bottom of a short staircase, the recruits stood in a crescent formation. Some chatted casually, others rubbed their hands excitedly, while still others pointed in my direction and rolled their heads in a sort of dismal way. This last group bothered me most of all.

My helper's arm slipped away, and I shifted my weight against the doorjamb, having no intention of taking so much as one more step. I wouldn't have either, except that a hand in the middle of my back urged me forward. I descended the stairs one at a time, feeling as forlorn as ever in my life.

Once past the shade of the overhang, the roof's protection vanished in a flash of sunlight. Superheated air enclosed me, along with a surrounding wall of faces, most with bright eyes and leering grins. No doubt the bored-to-death recruits would get some much awaited entertainment finally. What I wouldn't give to be among them, watching some other poor slob tremble and shake.

The Commander stepped from the ranks. Judging by his rows of white teeth, my suffering would increase by having to endure more of his untimely teasing.

"It's our two-for-one sale, laddy," he said, with a twinkle in his eyes. "Buy the first coffin and get the second for free."

A joke! At a time like this? Did the man have no feelings? Was I supposed to fall to the ground holding my ribs? Was there no sympathy, no caring, no compassion? Even more amazing than any of that, after a lifetime of conditioning, I actually smiled back or tried to.

"Cheer up, sport," the Commander chuckled. "And what flavor of embalming fluid would you prefer—lemon or peppermint?"

I couldn't believe it. Who was he anyway? Was the man even human?

Ju sighed aloud as if to make sure everyone listening understood he had done his darndest to inject a lighthearted touch. "I've always said you're far too grave, mate, and I see that hasn't changed. Not in the mood for a bit of levity, I take it?"

How insightful. Was I now supposed to admire such sensitivity?

"Dear me, lad, whatever possessed you to wave the red cape and get this mad bull pawing the dirt? Had you no idea how dangerous the brute is?"

"I—I didn't mean to, sir."

Ju put a comforting hand on my shoulder. "Here, there, steady that lip, mate, and don't you worry one bit. Should he try and make you linger, I'll step in and insist on his finishing the task. There'll be no dragging out agony on my watch." He lowered his voice so only I could hear, "Bit of humor once again, old boy. Oh, all right, I confess it was a poor show of taste. Habit, you know. Sorry about that."

His apology shocked me. Up until then I thought him incapable. Was this then a sign of hope? Would he cancel the fight? A commander could pull rank, couldn't he?

"Now to the contest, Tim-boy. Your being new to the camp, let me expound on the regulations for such a challenge as this. There are none."

My hopes sank to their lowest point yet.

"A bit of fun, old boy. Sorry. Actually, there are two rules. First, you as the one challenged get your choice of fighting instruments. Should you forfeit that selection, your opponent may then choose, and you elect the field of the battle. After you make a choice, it cannot be altered. Once the challenge is issued, there's to be no more speaking between fighters as everything must be handled through an intermediary, namely me." He leaned closer as if to have a word in private. "My advice, mate, is to pick weapons. Choose a long-range device in order to end the unhappy finish quickly, like pistols or rifles, even artillery—no, I'm not serious on the last one. Too messy. Anyway, choose something that'll eliminate any drawn-out suffering. This fiend," he said aside with a wink, "is a bloody connoisseur at inflicting pain."

From behind the Commander, Centipede stepped out of the formation wearing a smile that showed mostly gums and generally looked confident, as if he'd already won. I envied his self-assurance. He shed his buckskin shirt and threw a victorious wave to all the recruits. For being so tall and gangly, his muscled chest flared upward from a tiny waist like the flared hood of a cobra.

"Good show then," Ju continued, still talking to me. "Since you're the one who's been challenged, it's your call to say what's to be as far as fighting gadgets. Go on now, what'll it be? Here, go on," he prompted after not getting a response. "We're waiting your selection. Choose! Oh, chivvy along now," he urged. "Are you prepared to make first choice or not?"

Distrusting my voice for fear it would crack, I pointed at Centipede.

"Dear Gussey!" Ju gasped. "Don't do this, I say. You let him choose and you'll regret it. Upon my word, he'll pick bare hands, and you'll die most primitively."

I nodded at Centipede again, not wanting to point and expose my trembling.

The Commander groaned. As he predicted, the strapping fellow chose bare-handed.

"That's done then," the black man sighed, shaking his head. "Where's the battle to be conducted, lad?"

I aimed a wobbly finger in the direction of the gangly leader, only slightly higher this time, above his small head, at the massive gray object that'd been outside the mess hall window. The Commander turned, following my point. Centipede looked next. The whole assembly wheeled around. Everyone gasped at once.

"Blimey!" The Commander looked back down at me, frowning. "A jest, eh, lad? You don't mean to say *there*? Not that? You can't be serious?"

I nodded.

"Way up there?"

I nodded again.

"But the water tower? Why, no one could scuffle atop that tank. A bloke couldn't keep to his feet on such a steep slope, much less have a go at one another. You'll both tumble off."

This time I pointed down.

"*Inside!* Merciful saint's alive! Have you gone daft? Why, the bloody tank's full of toxic water. That's what shut the village down, don't you know. That alkaline stuff must be bitter as acid. Any sores will sting like fire and if one of you opens an eye, it'll melt in the socket. Should you swallow a mouthful, you'll end up salted herring."

"Not me." I found my voice at last.

Ju chuckled. "My dear chap, I must inform you, your opponent can't swim."

"I can."

Ju raised a skeptical eyebrow. "I say," he whispered, leaning in close, "is this a bluff?"

"No bluff."

He motioned at Centipede. The two stepped away together. They spoke in low tones. I watched both look toward the water tank, contemplate a moment, and resume the hushed conversation. The conference over finally, the Commander stepped back near me.

"The poor boy's lost his swagger, it seems. He requested another locale; that he's agreeable to anywhere you want but up there. He confided to me that he's a tad lacking at the crawl." Ju winked.

"Tell him I'm not." I'd heard exactly what I'd hoped for. "Tell him I've won the Fourth of July races at the country club every year. I even won a ribbon for holding my breath under water so long the lifeguards said my parents must be catfish."

Commander cackled and returned to Centipede. After another conversation, he came back. "Oh, my, my, how awkward. Says he wants a change of rules. Says he won't do it, he can't. He's willing for you to choose both weapons and location—anywhere other than down inside that water tank. I say, old chap," he murmured under his breath, "don't trust him. Let him off, and he'll waylay you some other time when no one's around."

I took the warning to heart. While the entire camp served as witnesses, I had to force the battle, despite that going against my every instinct.

"Tell him, sir, it's easy to be brave when you have all the advantages; that bullies are never so valiant as when the other guy doesn't stand a chance; that I'm only asking to even the odds some. It's no victory to stomp someone who's helpless. Surely he'll admit that. All I'm asking is that he get out of his element. And yet, it's not like he doesn't have his same advantages. He still has size, strength, and fighting know-how, while I only can swim. But, if he's too much of a *coward*"—I said the last extra loud so the whole camp could hear—"then he can lie on his back and do a hundred sit-ups."

The Commander relayed the terms at full volume. As he did, Centipede's small face changed shades like a pale moon lowering in a red sunrise. After a brief discussion between the two, the Commander returned to me. "He accepts. Bravo, Lad."

CHAPTER 11
The Bitter Water Battle

THE WATER TOWER STOOD AT the end of town. An iron ladder ran up one metal leg past the painted-on death's-head to the top of the dome-rounded tank. Taller than a skyscraper, at least when viewed from below, the tank's slight tilt gave it an unsteady appearance.

A pair of recruits had already climbed the ladder and busily worked at removing whatever lid existed on top. The closer I got to the tower, with the entire camp on my heels, the smaller the reservoir shrank.

Back at the mess hall, when noticing the tank for the first time, I pictured myself swimming freestyle from one end to the other, avoiding a floundering Centipede. That, I now saw, applied only to the Z-shaped, Olympic pool at the country club at home, not to this water tower. Inside the small reservoir, only a little larger than a cattle tank, there'd be no swimming around at all. Plus, the water's depth couldn't be more than twenty feet, so Centipede would only have to tread water to reach the sides with his long, powerful arms.

What little self-confidence I'd managed to scrape up sank amid all sorts of new fears. What if the tank turned out half-full? Why hadn't that crossed my mind until now? How could I stay away from Centipede then? Worse yet, what if no water at all existed inside? We'd end up practically in each other's arms. I had an image of being trapped inside the dark metal ball with the vicious brute, trying to escape in thick, gooey mud. My reoccurring nightmare of running away in slow motion had come true. It was the last straw. The battle seemed lost before we began.

Centipede and I stripped down to our skivvies—he, the spitting image of Hercules while, compared to him, I doubled for a tribal native during famine. I put my shirt back on. Suddenly faint, I leaned against the leg of the water tank.

A manhole-cover-size metal plate slammed onto the ground, raising a massive puff of dust. I jumped clear, my heart pounding in my throat. The lid missed me by less than a foot. Commander climbed the ladder first, then Centipede, and last of all, me. At each rung, I watched the powerful calf muscles above my head tighten to the size of cannonballs. The higher we went, the lower my hopes sank.

Once on top, we overlooked the ghost town, the trailers, and a desert stretching as far as an ocean floor without water. The three of us gathered around the center hole as the recruits who'd removed the lid descended the ladder. The tank's rounded surface sloped ever steeper until dropping straight down, but, surprisingly, the tin-plating didn't feel hot to my bare feet. Did this mean there was water inside? Who knew? Besides being curved, the smooth outer shell had nothing in the way of ridges or seams to act as handholds that might stop a body from sliding toward the edge.

One look into the opening of the hatch relieved one worry at least. A foot or so below the rim lay a blackish liquid, if liquid it was. The surface didn't ripple or slosh, which struck me as odd as the two recruits on the ladder rocked the tank considerably. It seemed there ought to be some movement down there. Had the water turned solid over time? Was that possible? One thing for sure, judging by the stink rising out of the hole, whatever was inside had turned rotten.

"Whewee! What a stench," the Commander exclaimed, crab-stepping down the slope with his nose into the breeze. His boots cocked at such a severe angle, he looked to be standing on his ankles. "You know, lads," he said, his tone indicating another untimely wisecrack, "those know-it-all scientist boys say life began in such a muck as this, and I can see their point. Why, one whiff of this would wake up most any dead thing and make the blighter slither downwind. Let's give her a period to air out, shall we?"

The way the camp commander risked the edge scared me. Without him, there'd be no hope of a fair fight. I would've made a grab for him except that might mean we both would go skidding off. Instead, I sat down at the opening and gripped the edge with my legs. That way, if he did slip, I'd at least have a secure hold to try for his hand. The hot metal rim stung through my shorts, leaving me no choice but to take off my shirt and use it for a buffer. Being seated had the unexpected but welcomed effect that the Commander extended his hand for my enemy to help him back up. Now if both would only lose their footing, I'd lunge for the Commander—but no such luck.

Curious as to what might be down inside the dark hole, I leaned over, resting my shoulders on my thighs. Sunlight sparkled in eye-stabbing glints off what appeared to be solid tar. I stretched out one leg and lightly stepped down on a crust, cracking it with my weight. A slimy liquid seeped up from underfoot that felt warm as bathwater.

The next thing I knew, my whole body plunged into the warm, slippery depths. It didn't feel like water at all, more like simmering oil. My skin tingled unpleasantly. It took a second to realize who shoved me in—not until Centipede's small head partially eclipsed the opening.

One corner of my lips burned where a drop splashed and it tasted so salty that a shudder went through me. Fortunately, my head had not gone under, but unfortunately, the reason was that Centipede held my wrist. He now lifted me back out the opening. Even as I felt myself being towed up, it was clear this was no rescue attempt. The Commander's grinning face replaced Centipede's in the opening. "You have only yourself to blame, laddie, as it's your own fault."

If that had been meant as comfort, it failed miserably. For whatever reasons, though, Centipede stopped pulling me back out.

"You allowed your enemy to jump the gun, as you Yanks articulate so aptly," the Commander continued with a good humored glint in his eye. "Once you entered the tank, you began the contest and, legally, your opponent's within rights to pull you back out and fashion chess pieces of your bones, if it suits his fancy. I should've mentioned that rule, perhaps, but who knew you'd be so impetuous?"

My arm twisted in Centipede's grip and felt on the verge of snapping, but I didn't dare struggle for fear of the brine splashing into my eyes. Meanwhile, the Commander jabbered on like he was trying his hand at sports announcing.

"Your combatant has a quandary to solve, Tim-boy, and I think this joust will be one for the archives. The dilemma he's got himself into," he explained, "is that, in diving for your arm, he lost his balance and, at the present, is dangling off the edge. The bally beggar is hanging onto you as a lifeline and clawing with his other hand for some sort of handhold. Now then, if you could manage to dislodge your forearm at the elbow, you'll still have half an arm, but he'll lose his...Oh, blast! That is a shame. Sorry, old chap, you've dithered too long. The blighter's got his leg up. What a pity. If I were you, I'd consider gulping that bilge and calling this match a forfeit."

I felt myself being lifted through the opening again. Left with no choice but the unthinkable, I shut my eyes and mouth and somersaulted. While blowing bubbles out my nose to keep back the toxic water, I grasped Centipede's thick wrist and, placing both feet on either side of the opening, pushed off downward with all my strength. The maneuver, called a "flip-turn" during my July Fourth racing days, succeeded in catching my enemy off guard as a massive splash shook the entire structure.

He let go my arm. I rocketed down to the bottom of the tank into a slimy, spongy bed of loose flakes. The scales flew up around me as if I were inside a snow globe. My eyes and mouth still shut airtight, I flip-turned once more and sprang toward the surface, speeding through the deposit chips.

On breaking the surface, I slung my head back and forth, shaking off excess liquid while treading water blind, expecting an attack at any moment. When the danger of liquid running into my eyes passed, I risked a peek. The corners of my eyes stung, but I refused to wipe them. My blurred vision cleared in time to catch sight of Centipede halfway back out the opening. Despite how I would've loved to let him escape, this would only put me back in the losing column. It took no more than two strokes to reach him. I locked my arms around his narrow, slippery waist.

Centipede's desperate thrashing actually helped me hang on because he bent at the waist to poke one leg through the opening, allowing me to tighten my grip by curling my legs around his midsection. The tank rocked until it seemed the whole structure would topple over. Such a pitiful moaning and wailing echoed inside the walls, I almost felt sorry for him, but not quite.

Whether the metal rim was too hot to hang onto or whether my dead weight won out, after a huge splash, he shoved me down into the depths. I swam back to the bottom. My biggest worry in returning to the surface became not so much being overpowered by him, but being caught in a drowning victim's death grasp. Centipede, like most who can't swim, wouldn't venture below the surface, but this didn't entirely work to the good. He still had sole possession of the air, and I'd soon have to join him.

Even worse, the backwash off his kicking sent a current to the bottom, which then rebounded upward, dragging me with it, forcing me to expend precious energy staying down. The one thing I must not do was swim into Centipede, and yet how to avoid that when blind? No longer able to fight the rising undercurrent and nearing the end of my air, I pushed off for the surface.

The one thing I didn't want to do, I did, colliding into my enemy's powerful chest. He wrapped me in such a bear hug that struggling was useless. His strong arms tightened in a bone-crushing grip, squeezing out what little air was left in my lungs. Instead of my resisting him, I went limp. No longer buoyant, my dead weight sank us both. This had to terrorize the nonswimmer.

Centipede kicked viciously, trying to keep us afloat while I remained calm as an anchor. Sure enough, unable to stand going beneath the surface, he thrust me down so violently that I jetted to the bottom then sprang back upward, only this time I angled to the side, scraping against the tank wall. After breaking the surface, my lungs screamed for air, but

I fought off the craving until after I had shaken off the excess salty water. Then, and only then, did I grab two huge breaths, and dove back for the depths.

Centipede's panicky kicking and floundering sent currents swirling every which way, reminding me of my days bodysurfing off the Texas coast and how frightening it could be to be caught in a riptide. That gave me an idea.

I reached both arms above my head and waited. Almost immediately, one hand contacted a lower leg as thick as a horse's ankle. I locked onto it and jerked down. Such storm-tossed undercurrents resulted that it seemed the tank must surely burst its seams. My body whirled around as if caught in an undertow. Just when I could no longer hang on and flew against the tank wall, a strange calm settled throughout the water. After all the turbulence, the stillness made me shudder.

Panic-stricken at the idea of swimming into my enemy's grip again, I inched my way upward until I bumped into a suspended body. The floating figure didn't react. Using the massive shoulders as a springboard, I pushed off to the surface. Centipede no doubt had swallowed a toxic drink.

A pair of hands lifted me through the opening. Standing on the slippery surface became all but impossible because of my being dripping wet. I grasped the Commander while shivering and heaving great gulps of air.

"Well, well, here's a fish I didn't expect to beach," he exclaimed, cheerful as ever. "And so small a catch I suppose I ought to toss him back. Since you're under the legal limit, mate, I'll change bait and recast for... Here! Where you off to, lad?"

Unable to bear any more corny jokes, I started down the ladder, hanging onto the rail for dear life and taking one slick rung at a time. Once at ground level, I collapsed on the sand. A bucket of cool water crashed over my head, thanks to some kind soul. Not only was the dousing refreshing, but better yet, the bucketful washed off the stinging slime. After a second bucket, this time poured slowly onto my upturned face, my eyes quit burning and the blurriness cleared away.

Above me, Centipede's body was lowering. At the other end of the rope, the two recruits who'd taken off the lid had their feet braced against the ladder's top rung. A more hideous sight I'd never seen. The small oval-shaped face had yellowish-gray skin. Green liquid spilled out a slack jaw. He looked gruesomely full to the brim.

"Hurrah!"

The unexpected shout from behind caused me to shrink away, uncertain what the outcry meant. A crowd gathered around. Expecting to be set upon, I hadn't the strength to cover my head.

"Hurrah!"

Instead of raining down blows, a multitude of hands hoisted me to my feet, then up onto their shoulders. The recruits paraded me around the water tower like a football hero, all the while shouting, "Hurrah!"

Victor's multicolored truck passed by with the tailgate down and blue feet sticking out the back.

"Hurrah!" The cheers lifted even louder at the sight of the defeated leader. "Hurrah!"

None of us could know that our celebration would turn out premature.

CHAPTER 12
A New Camp Tyrant

AFTER WHAT BECAME KNOWN AS the Bitter Water Battle, a new tyrant arose to abuse the recruits, and with a temper that went off faster than Centipede's ever had. Never had there been seen in camp such a swaggering, fight-spoiling hothead. No one could say a word without this new ruffian analyzing the remark for offense. Challenge warnings were a daily event, although no actual fighting ever resulted because either the timing was bad or an injury prevented a fair contest or too many pressing duties that "couldn't wait" interfered. Consequently, although many threats got issued, no actual blood ever spilled.

Yes, sad to say, the new camp browbeater was none other than me. Overnight, I became the thing I most detested—a rough-talking, lapel-wadding bully, but who could blame me? Up until that moment, my bravest act had been to pick up an insect and now every tough guy around trembled in my presence. No one dared talk back to the victor of the Bitter Water Battle. Wasn't it only natural that such newfound respect went straight to my head? Thankfully, though, after a brief reign as "Camp Champ," my attitude changed suddenly. I returned to my same old, people-pleasing self.

At this same time, a rumor came around that Centipede had not died after all. He had instead, against all odds, made an amazing recovery in an Ojinaga hospital and was due back in camp any day. After making amends to anyone who'd accept my apology, a weight lifted off my shoulders. The life of a "scrapper," as we used to call schoolyard toughs, turned out to be a big disappointment. I once secretly envied bullies. It never entered my mind that such a position would end up so unhappy. I imagined that other guys would want to be like me, but it turned out just the opposite. I ended up alone and friendless. To be feared, I found out, means to be secretly despised.

Another rumor came around that greatly improved my life. I once again slept at night and my appetite returned. Birds sang in the morning, sunsets burst from behind the mountains gloriously, and the clear nighttime air became a delight to breathe. This latest gossip reported that Centipede developed pneumonia and wouldn't rejoin the camp after all. Instead, he must recover at his sister's home in Delicias. After the welcome news, I never returned to being the "Camp Champ," except for one last close call.

At the time, I'd been "having it out" with the carrot-topped recruit named Red. The show-off tried taking over for me as table cut-up during my brief rein as camp bully, but he lacked the talent. Instead of funny, he ended up annoying everyone, especially me. Finally, at one midday meal, I lost all patience.

"You dumb woodpecker!" I jumped up and threw my empty tin cup, which he ducked. "For little of nothing, I'd…" Suddenly coming to myself, I stood there like a fool, unable to think of what to say next. I'd almost relapsed. Once having gotten in the habit of losing my temper, it'd become almost impossible to stop. No one felt worse than me afterward, but that didn't help. "Look, Red, forget about it, okay? I don't know what came over me. I won't do it again, honest." That was a promise I wasn't sure I could keep.

Fear blazed in the redhead's eyes. "I didn't mean to offend, Leader."

Everyone started calling me that since the Bitter Water Battle. I tried to stop them after my change of heart, but they refused. "I know, I know. Don't worry, you didn't do anything wrong. I'm just on edge lately." Since I'd gained the ear of everyone at the table with my outburst, I thought here's a chance to unload and explain my recent misbehavior. Who knows, maybe they'd understand, and we could start back the way things used to be. "Look, guys, I realize I've been acting a jerk these days. You fellows are my best pals and I wouldn't do anything to hurt that, but I'm under a lot of pressure because, from all the signs, the Commander will soon ask me to take Centipede's place. He hasn't yet, I know, but he will because..." I started to say 'who else besides me has the reputation?' but decided against it. "To tell the truth, I don't want the position. I don't like pushing people around, but how can I refuse?"

"You take over for Centipede, Leader?" Red asked, not bothering to hide his surprise.

"Oh, don't worry, not *like* him." I saw a chance to really get in their good graces. "In fact, I would accept the position mostly for you guys. When I'm in charge, I won't forget anyone. As the saying goes, 'All boats are lifted with a rising tide.' I'll not only remember you, but we'll each share in whatever benefits there are together."

"Pardon my interrupting, Leader," Red put in, "but you needn't worry so. I heard this morning that new leadership from outside the camp is coming."

This took me back. "Who says?"

"Didn't you hear the loud noise last night?"

"You mean, thunder?"

"Not thunder. It never rains here. An airplane."

"Yes," the recruit next to him agreed. A hatchet-faced kid with a nose like a beak, he had only recently joined our table. "I helped set up the runway lights."

"They are most important men, too," Red put in, after flashing the new recruit a resentful glance as if it was his story to tell. "From South America."

"South..." That really took me back. "How you know that?"

"They had a conference this morning with the Commander. I worked outside the trailer replacing the steps with railroad ties. Their voices went through the thin metal wall so I could hear every word. The men say they plan to bring back the one who began these camps. A man by the name of Acey Elu. They argued, too. The Commander wanted more time to prepare, saying the recruits he handpicked to send weren't fully trained yet, but the men from South America say he must bring Acey Elu back now, no matter what."

I should have felt disappointed perhaps, although a troubling question did come to mind. Would Red overstate such news in order to get back at me for scolding him? There was only one way to find out. "Tell me everything you heard. Don't leave out anything."

"Certainly, Leader. The men talk very much about this man, Acey Elu. I hear them say he begins in Chicago, but during World War II, he runs away to escape being drafted in the army and ends up in Colombia, South America. In 1948, when there is much anger in a city called Bogota, he reappears in time to start Bogotazo. Have you heard of this?"

"No."

"It is a most famous event to ever happen in South America. In Bogotazo many relatives of mine were wiped out. I hear the men this morning say that this man, Acey Elu, is the one who begins Bogotazo. He hires an assassin to shoot another man called Jorge Eliecer Gaitan, a very popular politician. Bogota erupts in a riot that continues to this day. The city was destroyed until the army seized control. The generals cannot stop the revolution, though, that spreads throughout Colombia to become La Violencia. Many hundred thousand die, but Acey Elu gets away and goes to Mexico to start camps to train new fighters. He writes books that spread his ideas worldwide. Those in sympathy with him send support. However, the job proves too great for him with many, many problems. He has a nervous breakdown and disappears from Mexico. They say he shows up again in Texas at a place by the name of Big Spring State Hospital."

"*Big Spr*—I know that place!" I could hardly believe it. "It's not far from where I grew up. Big Spring, Texas. But it's no hospital. It's a nuthouse where they lock up crazy people. It's more a prison than a hospital. The place is away from civilization, and people who commit the worst crimes get sent there. This guy, what's his name?"

"Acey Elu."

"Wait a minute, I think I may have heard of him. Before I left home, all the kids in my town had a curfew to be off the streets because of a lunatic mass-killer that ran away from that place you're talking about. Maybe this guy, Acey Elu, is the same one."

"Yes, the men from South America say that he has escaped."

"But I still don't get it. If he's so crazy, why bring him back here?"

"Donations, the men say. Contributors support Acey Elu and him only. They send money from all over the world. Many countries also. These men tell Commander that since Acey Elu is no longer part of movement, contributions steadily drop. Finances are very bad. The South Americans tell the Commander he must send some men to get Acey Elu and bring him back. They say they have no choice."

"Well, well." I sighed. "Maybe I won't be taking over the camp after all."

"Does this mean, Leader," Red asked, with a wide grin, "you're going back to telling jokes and doing your tricks?"

"Why not?" I felt like my old self again finally, except for one not-too-small concern. "If this Acey Elu turns out like you say, we may wish Centipede had come back after all." I forced a laugh, but it sounded fake.

Later that afternoon, word came around that the Commander wanted to see me in his office. Despite everything, I still worried he would offer me Centipede's old position. Why else would he want to see me? But what could I say? The only reason I'd even think about accepting would be to gain freedom to find Hect. Otherwise, the idea of throwing my weight around and bossing everyone sickened me. Then again, it may not be allowed to turn down such a promotion. I hadn't spoken to the Commander since the day of the Bitter Water Battle but knew all about his reputation for having things "his way."

Headquarters offices occupied one end of the mess hall with an entryway at the backside of the trailer. The outside couldn't have looked less impressive. Newly stacked railroad ties replaced a rusted-out metal staircase left to one side. Yellowing tape pieces covered the door, left over from messages that had since been removed. While waiting to be called in, the surprise of my life strolled up. "Hect!"

"Hi," he said, as calm as if we'd seen each other yesterday. "How you been?"

"Er, fine." It felt awkward like two strangers meeting. "And you?"

"Not bad." He shaded his eyes with his hand against the bright sun.

The reserved greeting not only set me back, but, adding to my shock, my best friend looked all but unrecognizable. His body had slimmed down, and his hair had grown out bushy on top with burred sides that lengthened his once-round face. I hardly knew what to say next. "Hect, is that you?"

"You can see, can't you?" he said sourly as if that'd been a dumb question. "So then, you didn't die in the desert after all."

"No. No, I didn't." All but tongue-tied, I could barely think. "You're right."

"A long walk, I bet."

"Very." Nothing made sense. He didn't act glad to see me at all. Should I tell him that he'd been the reason I'd come all the way out here? How could he not know? Our meeting so far felt like we had never known each other. "I...I worried I might not find you."

"Worried? Why's that?"

"Well..." Who was this person anyhow? Not Hect, at least not the easy-going kid I once knew. He acted so direct and sort of cut-and-dried. And there was something else different about him even beyond his looks or his curtness, but I couldn't put my finger on it. I never felt so ill at ease. "To see if you were all right."

"I'm fine. So, how'd your little adventure in the desert go?"

"My *adventure*?" Had I heard right? Was he kidding? "I'd hardly call it an adventure."

"Not dramatic enough, huh?"

"Dra—!" I gulped down a rising anger. "I would've still been out there buried in the sand if you double-crossers on the truck had your way. It was no walk in the park, let me tell you. How come you guys drove off and left me out there to die like that?"

"Aw, there's no need to exaggerate."

I couldn't think straight. The hairs on the back of my neck seemed to stick straight out. "You sorry scamps abandoned me with no water, no food, and lost as I could be, plus no shade from a fiery sun."

"Here, ain't no use'n you gettin' on no high hors..." He cleared his throat. "I mean, there's no reason to raise your voice. Cool down."

Now I knew what was different about him. What happened to his country accent? How'd he lose it? And why? The realization took my anger away. After all, I should be glad to see my best friend, right? So what if he acts a little different? We'd just gotten off on the wrong foot, is all. "I'm sorry, Hect. You're right. I didn't mean the name-calling."

"That's better. You always was...or, *were* a hothead."

Despite the huffy return, something more important caught my ear. When Hect lost his temper, he'd sounded like his old self again. Did that mean beneath that phony stuff, my best friend still existed? If only I knew what happened to make him different. Who changed him? Because of this, I rephrased my question. "I was just curious why you guys didn't come back for me in the desert, that's all."

"If you'd give me a chance to explain without flying off the handle, I'll tell you. Shoot-fire, you ain't...or *haven't* changed a bit, have you?" He drew a calming breath. "Anyhow, like I was saying, the ride that night was plenty rough, if you recall. Me and—or rather, the Commander and I didn't even know you'd fallen off the truck. Once we did notice, despite us banging on the cab, the driver wouldn't stop. When he finally did, he told us he felt the truck wheels run over you. A lie, obviously, but how could we know that at the time?"

"Who was the driver?"

"The recruit leader."

"Centipede, that figures. No wonder he never liked me. My arriving at camp like I did showed him up for a liar."

"Can I finish?" Hect said, a little peeved.

"Sure."

"Centipede, as you call him, finished by saying that if we went back for you, anyone chasing us would discover the location of the camp. Plus, he was under direct orders not to depart from the planned escape route. And that's why we didn't come back."

"Well, I did survive, no thanks to...oh, forget it." Despite the explanation, which I had to admit sounded reasonable, I still smarted over his attitude. "I thought us better pals, that's all."

"Dadblamed fool, how many times I got'ta tell y...I mean, there's no use in going over this anymore. What's done is done. Why not tell me what happened instead?"

He deserved a dose of the silent treatment, but I went ahead and told him about wandering in the desert, about battling Blacky and the other scorpions, about repairing the windmill, and about Half-Ear and the other two mules taking me to the farmhouse that belonged to Bernardo and Maria. I finished by telling him about Juarez, the girl with the flat face, Raul stealing Victor's truck, and our following the tire tracks.

Talk about a letdown. For all the interest he showed, yawning and looking around, I may as well have said nothing at all. For the life of me, I couldn't figure out who my onetime friend had become. Didn't he care anymore? Had he no feelings? "Hect, you know, I came all the way out here to find you."

"Needn't'ov...I mean, you didn't need to. I'm fine."

I sat down on the edge of a step leading up to the trailer and picked up a dead Yucca leaf, fanning my hot face. "Oh, great. What's that supposed to mean?"

"It means, you wasted your time coming out here. I'm content as ever."

"You can't mean that. In *this* place? Wouldn't you like to go back home and finish high school? Maybe learn a trade."

He stiffened noticeably. "I might'a knowed you..." He stopped midsentence and took a deep breath. "I should've known you would offer something like that. That's all your kind think people like me are capable of—a trade."

That's the first I ever heard anything like that from him. "What's 'my kind' mean?"

"Rich folks. Worse yet, *born* rich. Everything's been handed to you your whole life so it's natural to think in those terms about someone like me. Learn a trade, get a blue-collar job, mow lawns, scratch out a living as a janitor or a trash man, that's all you can do anyhow."

"Now you know what I'm thinking, do you?" My blood pressure was rising again. "Where'd all that come from?"

"I learned a lot since I seen...or *saw* you last. There's a big difference between us. You'll go to a fine university, maybe flunk out once or twice, but what's it matter? You'll still inherit your folk's pile of dough and live off the cream while hiring me to fix your car or paint your house. No wonder you want me to learn a trade."

That stumped me. How to counter that? My best pal had learned some strange ideas. "What's happened to you, Hect? You're not the same person. I don't even know how to talk to you anymore. What's going on?"

"I've been taught what you and your kind are about, that's what. And if any of the boys around here knew what I know, you'd be in for a rough time of it. There are no rich boys here, far from it. We're all working class or less, but don't worry, I won't tell. After all, you made the trip out here to try and do me a favor, I'll grant you that."

I couldn't have felt more at a loss. Here I'd left everything and come all the way out here, and for what? For this? How much better off would things have been at military school—with an allowance, school holidays, summers off, instead of being trapped in a mercenary army where "my kind" were hated. Was this the price to pay for disobeying my parents?

The Commander leaned out the door, looking snappy as ever in his uniform and tall black boots, with a dagger and scabbard on his hip. This last item left me wondering. Why a weapon way out here in the middle of nowhere? He motioned us to step inside.

Once in front of his desk, Hect and I stood side by side at attention. While the Commander shuffled papers, I stole a look around.

His office appeared even more unimpressive inside. Narrow and cramped, with no personal items, not even pictures on the wall. Even his desk at one time had been a picnic table, and it took up half the room, leaving barely enough space at one end for a person to sidle by. The

Commander leaned back in a four-legged chair against the wall, crossing his feet on the desk edge. He wore his ever-present, half-cocked smile.

"Tim-lad," he began, withdrawing the dagger and aiming it at me, "I'll not soon forget the day you engaged in that underwater tussle at the water tower—Genghis Khan Tactics versus modern submarine warfare, eh?" He grinned, exposing pearl white teeth.

His comment seemed unremarkable enough at first, but after the black man kept staring with wide-eyed expectancy, it dawned on me the remark had not been offhand. He had prepared it, perhaps with no small amount of thought. Too late to laugh, though, the silence hung awkwardly.

The man's face fell at last. "Oh, bosh! You two remain in a dour mood, I see. In which case we may as well get down to business. I've a top-secret mission for you both to perform. It's all very hush-hush, high security, a spy-type undertaking. You're to be my secret agents, if you will."

Not about to miss another punch line, I let out a high-spirited whoop and nudged Hect with an elbow to join in. The Commander's scowl stopped me short.

"Something bloody comical, mate?"

The warmth drained out of my face. "Oh. No...I guess not, sir."

His feet slid off the desk edge, and he half stood, his fists on the desktop. "Then you will kindly control the urge to bray like a mule in a meeting of vital importance, no matter how strongly the instinct of that ignoble beast comes upon you."

"I—I...that is...I'm sorry. I thought you might be joking."

"Joking, is it? At a time such as this? The problem with you, recruit, is you must learn when the proper occasion for humor is and when it's improper. Blokes of your ilk have flawed timing, if you want the fact of the matter. Our situation couldn't be more serious and you act like we're sitting around a campfire swapping anecdotes."

I started to apologize again when the corners of the man's lips twitched; his face contorted; he sputtered; and finally broke into a fit of laughter. "Just pulling the old peg leg, Tim-boy. Having a bit of fun at your expense, get me? Don't take it serious."

Thoroughly shaken, I didn't know how to react. Never in my life had I been so thrown off balance by such a peculiar personality. His weird sense of humor left me no firm footing to know when to take him seriously and when not to.

"Now then, as I was saying before being interrupted." He winked at me and tilted back his chair, crossing his feet again. "That night in the Juarez lockup, I handpicked you two for this job. You subsequently gave me a bit of a start, Tim-lad, when you instigated that tussle at the water tower. All my planning seemed destined to go down the drain, if you get the pun, but not to worry, as things worked out to both our liking. Anyway, before I go into detail about your mission, I need to brief you on a bit of background data. It has no doubt caught your eye that the rest of the lads around here come from Latin countries while some have European backgrounds. You and Hect are among our early American arrivals. Since we're an international organization, everyone must be fluent in a common language, which we've determined will be English. Hect here has done a smashing job improving his grammar, by the by."

I wanted to look at my friend, but didn't dare. So that's it. That's what became of his country accent.

"All the lads," the Commander continued, "are being trained to return to their original country one day and be accepted into the very top echelons of society. Now to tell you a little about our venture, I personally think of it as the Eliza Doolittle project. The name comes from my favorite British play *Pygmalion* by George Bernard Shaw. You're no doubt familiar with it?"

Hect and I gave each other lost looks.

"Ah—hem, yes, not your bailiwick perhaps." His smile dipped briefly, but then returned. "Suffice it to say our rough-edged, uncultured recruits will be refined under our care until the most elite of their respective societies cannot tell the difference. You most certainly are asking yourselves, why train them here in the middle of the desert? Good question. The answer is quite simple: Mexico happens to be the most accommodating place to establish multinational camps such as ours. The government cares less about these desert wastelands and leaves us alone."

My mind kept trying to wander, but I forced it to focus.

"Am I boring you, Tim-lad?"

"No, sir!"

After a skeptical sigh, the Commander uncrossed and recrossed his feet. "The mission I have for you lads requires two authentic, red-blooded Yank teenagers. None of the recruits around here are sufficiently, oh, how shall I say it, *Americanized*? This task requires ingenuity of the most agile sort, a confidence born in privilege, plus that brash Yank cocksureness. Such traits cannot be taught to peasants who've been shuffled around all their lives. I say all this because you may find yourselves stopped by Border Patrols, in which case it will call for improvisation on your part. Otherwise, you'll blend in well enough with all the other American teenagers headed for a night at 'Boystown,' as they call the nightclub district. Chances are the guards won't give you a second glance, as there are far too many young reprobates on Friday and Saturday nights. However, now for the crucial part of the mission."

Ju rose to his feet. Compared to his overbearing presence, his small size always threw me. He pulled down a map from a tube on the wall. The map showed south Texas and northern Mexico. "Here we are in the state of Chihuahua." He placed the tip of his dagger blade over a spot in the upper portion of Mexico. "Over here at this tiny speck of a town just this side of the border is a low-water crossing on the Rio Grande with a rock bottom easily traversed by vehicle when the water is down, like now." He stuck the knife blade through the map into the wall at a point midway in the long Mexico-Texas border. "Boquillas del Carmen, the town is called. Directly across from it, on the other side of the river, is Big Bend National Park. Once you have navigated the park, you'll drive north on 385 and then west on 19 to a town called Van Horn, Texas. At an address I'll give you, a chap will be waiting by the name of Acey Elu."

CHAPTER 13
Across the Border

HOW I KEPT FROM JUMPING straight out of my shoes, who knew. Could there be two of them? With such an unusual name, it didn't seem possible. Acey Elu had to be one and the same. I edged over closer to Hect and, as the Commander faced the map, gave him an elbow. He returned a scowl and backed away. A knock at the trailer door caused us both to stiffen.

"I'm in a meeting," the Commander called over his shoulder.

"Pardon, sir," a muffled voice returned. "It's important."

"When is it not?" he mumbled and squeezed past the desk and wall. "I'll be back in short order, lads."

As soon as the door shut, Hect looked at me like he was about to throw a punch. "What's wrong with you? He already knows you're not listening. Don't drag me along with you into trouble and make him think I'm not paying attention either."

"Listen!" I didn't dare speak above a whisper. "I know that guy."

"Who?"

"Acey Elu, I've heard of him. He's a killer. He's one craz—"

"Shhh-hhtt!"

Despite the shushing, I couldn't stop. "No, listen! The man's a real wacko revolutionary, totally nutso. He's been responsible for the deaths of thou—"

The trailer door opened.

"Hear this!" The Commander said, reentering the office. He once again scooted past the tight squeeze between desk and wall. "Never, *ever* talk to him. Ever!"

I was stunned. How had he heard? I couldn't have kept my voice any lower. The trailer walls weren't that thin. Was the place bugged? Whatever the answer, Hect didn't deserve to get in trouble along with me. Things between us were bad enough already. I had to speak up. "Sorry, sir. It's my fault, not his."

"Fault?" The man turned back from the map, looking puzzled. "What's your fault?"

"Talking." I nodded in the direction of my friend. "I talked to him, not him to me."

"Blimey! What are you bothering about now, lad?"

"It's me. I'm to blame. You said not to talk, but it was me, not him, that talked."

"No, no, not you. Acey Elu. Do not speak to *him*. He will most certainly attempt to engage you in dialog—that cannot be prevented—but under no circumstances are you to respond. Pretend you don't hear, ignore him, be rude if you must, but do not answer."

I wasn't sure I heard right? "Not at all, sir?"

"Ever! And I'll tell you why. Acey Elu is daft. A schizoid. Crackerjacks. The bloke talks to himself, communes with unseen voices, and lives in a world of his own making."

I had an inkling of that already, having heard as much at the mess hall table from Red and the guys, but it sounded ten times worse hearing it confirmed.

"As long as you chaps don't talk to him, he's harmless," the Commander went on. "Most likely, he won't even notice you're around. Normally, he mumbles to himself and keeps his own company, and generally isn't aware of other blokes even if they're right there with him face to face."

Nothing made sense. Then why go after the loon? Who needs another crackpot?

"But the man's a genius," he explained, as if in answer to my thoughts. "Before his mental breakdown, these camps were his inspiration. Even today, his writings, his philosophy, and his opinions on political matters have achieved notable popularity."

That puzzled me even more. What possible popular philosophy could a nutcase offer?

"His doctrines are quite involved, and we haven't time to discuss them in depth here, but you'll be required to study his writings soon enough. His top seller is a book that encompasses in a nutshell his philosophy."

Curious, I couldn't keep from asking. "What book, sir?"

"It's one entitled *We Know Best*."

"Excuse me, sir, I don't mean to be a bother, but who are the 'We'?

"You lads may not fully realize it yet at such a young age, but John Q. Public is a trifle dull—lacks willpower, is unruly, undisciplined, unable to control his appetites, and generally immoderate. The average Joe is little above virtual tribesmen in moral fiber and needs looking after in the worst way. So, Acey Elu has made it his mission to insist they do what they should, like it or not. That's who the 'We' are."

The next question followed naturally. "Pardon me, sir, I don't mean to intrude, but what is it that the 'We' then 'Know Best'...if I may ask."

"Everything, lad." The Commander answered as if that should've been perfectly obvious. "In the book, Acey Elu presents himself as a strict-but-caring father who must restrain the undisciplined impulses of his wayward, willful populace."

I wanted to know more, but feared my questions were a distraction.

"But back to my previous point, I can't stress enough that you not talk to Acey Elu. To emphasize my point, allow me to tell you the fate of the last driver who ignored my cautions. Unable to endure the constant string of opinions, several of which he took issue with, he finally broke down and countered with a conviction of his own. True to my warning, offense was taken and his rider kicked the driver's seat from behind so violently the steering column drove into the poor bloke's chest cavity. I must say, we

100

had a dickens of a time getting his remains off of that contraption, too. So, keep mum."

Hect and I traded stricken looks.

"Dear Gussie," the man suddenly exclaimed. "You've both gone pallid. Aren't either of you proud? I handpicked you lads for this assignment. Cheer up. Don't you realize I'm giving you the chance of a lifetime? You'll end up champions."

I'd heard that term before, but "champion" no longer held the same appeal. The title had lost all its power to make me want to be one.

"Perhaps you lads will feel more favorable when you discover who's due back tomorrow." He paused a moment. "Your old water-tower opponent, Tim-lad."

I managed not to gasp *"Centipede!"* Even more alarming was the news that he'd be back tomorrow. I knew one day his return would happen, but hoped for more time to prepare. At least I'd retired my position as "Camp Champ" and didn't have to defend that title, hopefully.

"I thought as much," the Commander said with a satisfied tone. "The bloke's mucked around and made a miraculous recovery. Any postponement of his return is impossible. My plan, then, is to get you lads out of here before he makes you into a useful product like, oh, say, fertilizer." He yelped at this, but stopped when we didn't join in. "Look at it this way, lads. Should you complete this most urgent mission successfully and return intact, no one would dare attempt revenge on two camp heroes."

I seriously doubted that anything could persuade Centipede to back off now, but he said something else that got my attention even more— "return intact." Was that his way of saying we might not return in one piece? Why? Because of the mission? Or the madman?

From there on, the meeting consisted of particulars about our trip. He finished by warning us to be careful not to miss the turnoff to Boquillas del Carmen. Otherwise, we'd end up in Ojinaga and her sister city, Presidio, Texas. Although a much faster and easier way to go, it was also one that led to a border crossing inspection station. There, we'd be stopped, possibly interrogated, and maybe even inspected, so we were to avoid the bridge at all costs.

I barely listened because of thinking about Acey Elu, who I had no intention of ever meeting up with. Still, who wouldn't wonder what might have been? If I'd actually met the monster, could I have ignored him? Did I have the backbone, especially if he spoke directly to me? The answer, of course, was no way. Either my resolve would break down, or I'd have a forgetful lapse, and say something. Thankfully, I wouldn't find out. The bloodthirsty revolutionary and I would never meet, no chance, not in a thousand years—if everything went right, that is.

CHAPTER 14
Acey Elu

~~~

THE OVER-SIZED STATION WAGON THE Commander assigned to us had at one time been an ambulance during World War II, judging by its olive green color and the outline of a Red Cross on its side. Two-door with knobby, truck tires, the Dodge had a jump seat in back inside a large cargo space. We loaded our supplies into the rear double doors, five-gallon cans of fuel, plus K-rations that'd been packaged in the 1940s probably, water jugs, and tools for any breakdowns.

Hect was put in charge, which wouldn't have bothered me as he had been at camp longest, except for the change in personality of my one-time best friend. Could he still be trusted? If we got in a tight spot, would he back me up like he used to when we grew up together, or leave me stranded like he did in the desert? Since I no longer belonged to his "kind of folks," as he called it, who knew.

After we'd loaded up, the Commander took us both aside. "You'll be watched along the way, lads, so fasten this warning in the forefront of your minds—meander very little."

That, of course, brought up an obvious question. "What if we get lost, sir?"

"You've a map." The man's ever-present half smile dropped away. "Follow it. Don't stop, turn around, or deviate for any reason. Excuses will not be accepted."

On that worrisome send-off, we drove out of camp into the desert. I, as navigator, poured over the map, checking and rechecking every turn, road sign—what few there were—and any landscape highlights. Not only that, but I kept one eye on the dashboard compass as if our lives depended on it, which may well have been the case. When not absorbed by all that, I worried over Hect. Why did he act so solemn? Not one word had passed between us so far. Underneath his unfriendliness, did my onetime pal still exist? Can a person change so drastically like that? And in such a short time? Was it an act? How to get him to let down his defenses? When we came to a straightaway paved road, I could relax my navigating, and decided to find out. "Hey, Hect,—"

"'Sir,' you mean."

I sat upright. "You're kidding?"

"You heard the Commander. I outrank you."

"Aw, come on, Hect. What's with you?"

"'What's with you—*what?*"

I had no intention of saying sir. "It's me, Hect, your best friend. I came out here to rescue you—at no small amount of trouble, not to mention being beat up by a couple of thugs guarding the camp."

"Who asked you?" He glanced over with a cutting look. "And what gave you the notion I want rescued?"

He had me there. I'd never thought of that, but I still had an ace in the hole. "You will once you hear what I have to say. It's my little secret. The reason I came all the way out here was to tell you that we didn't commit a crime, after all. Actually, we *solved* one by burning down the shack. And there wasn't any hobo inside either. The place was full of dummies. Mannequins. Some dress-shop owner tried to hide her inventory out there after she set her building in town on fire. We got a reward." I let the excitement build. "You and I, a thousand bucks each! In the bank, just waiting for us back home." I didn't mention that my share was gone.

"So?"

"'*So?*' Are you crazy? Hect, a thousand bucks! In the bank. One solid grand, all yours, just waiting there, didn't you hear me? All for you."

"It don't matter non...I mean, it doesn't matter."

Talk about a letdown. There had to be a misunderstanding. "Hect, we're talking hard, cold cash. Enough one-dollar bills to fill up a suitcase." I didn't know how else to explain it. "That's one hundred one-hundred dol—"

"I know, I know," he snapped. "I'm not dumb, despite what you think. You can't get it through that thick head of yours that I finally found a home. No amount of money can buy that. This place is where I belong. You think I'd leave all this for money?"

"But, Hect, think about what you just said—all this? We're in some kind of renegade militia outfit, or mercenary army, whatever, who knows what to call it, but there's no one in their right mind who would call it home."

"Not for you, rich boy, but what've I got to go back to? No family, no future, nothing. I ain't going nowheres...I mean, I'm not going anywhere. This is my home. Here, I have a future. Even better, one day I'll be somebody, just you watch. It's only a matter of time, my instructors say."

Things started to make sense for once. So that's it. Come to think of it, what *did* he have to go back to? Still, I had one more trump card left. "Okay, okay, maybe so. I don't get it completely, but have it your way. Only this next item will convince you for sure. You don't know who we've been sent to pick up. I do. That's what I tried to tell you in the Commander's office. This fellow, Acey Elu, is a real nutcase. Some guys at camp told me about him. He's been penned up in Big Spring State Hospital, and you know about that place. Not only that, but he was the leader of some sort of rebellion in South America. The Commander acted like he's a little strange, that's all, but don't you believe it. He's a full-blown maniac, a killer."

"The Commander has his reasons for sending us," Hect said, calm as could be. "If he wants this fellow picked up, that's what we'll do."

The air went out of me on that one. That'd been my last shot, leaving me without anything. If I didn't know who Hect was before, he seemed from another planet now. With all my arguments defeated, what else was there but to plead? "But, Hect, once we crossed the border, I thought we would head to West Texas. This may be our only chance to escape."

"Don't you try it," he warned no longer the least bit calm. He swerved to miss a mashed skunk in the road. The strong odor invaded our cab's interior. "You do, and I'll stop you. Don't make me do it. You try anything, I'll stop you flat."

That did it. I washed my hands of trying to talk sense to him. "Okay, you want to stay, go ahead, but not me. I'm going home."

"No, you ain't...*aren't*."

"You mean—" This was the biggest shock of all. "You won't let me go?"

"Right! You mess me up on this mission, my career's over. I have this one chance to make good and show the Commander what I can do. Don't you even think of leaving."

I hardly knew what to say after that. Now what was I to do? "But what about me? I came all the way out here to tell you you're innocent of any crime and that you've got a thousand bucks in the bank. I thought you'd be glad."

"Look, I know you think we're still pals, like we used to be. We ain— We're not. Far from it."

Two buzzards beside the road having rabbit dinner flew off in different directions.

"We're enemies," Hect continued. "It's on account of you and people like you that I've never had a chance in life. For a long time, I didn't know better, but my eyes have been opened. Up till now, it's all been you rich boys' way. Now it's my turn."

As I watched, the two buzzards flew so gracefully, both making wide circles on their way back behind us to their meal. Who had Hect become? Whoever he was, he sure had left me in a lurch. Not only had my getaway plans been ruined, but I couldn't go back to camp either because of Centipede. As bad as I hated to chauffeur Acey Elu, what other choice did I have?

At an unpaved road leading off to the right, I forced myself to put all that aside and get back to my job as navigator. According to the map, we had to cut across open desert to Boquillas del Carmen. A more barren and uninhabited countryside seemed impossible to imagine. On the other hand, the map showed a paved, two-lane highway "Camino 67" traveling straight north to the sizable town of Ojinaga and its sister city, Presidio, Texas. As near as I could guess, we had a hundred-and-fifty-mile detour of wilderness. After my previous experience being lost in the desert, I considered waylaying my onetime friend and taking over, but couldn't bring myself to do it.

We turned east and drove in a dust cloud, arriving hours later at a fork in the road called Ejido El Guaje. The place reminded me of a Navajo village from a Western movie. One house had a sign that read "SE VENDE GASOLINA," so we filled up an almost empty tank, paying with the pesos the Commander gave us for traveling money and saving our own gasoline for later. For a few pesos more, we got tacos and two bottles of Pulque—a milky drink with quite a kick.

From there, we drove on until late afternoon, when we arrived at a line of salt cedars marking the Rio Grande. Our presence considerably increased the population of Boquillas del Carmen from the look of the empty streets and abandoned buildings. How anyone survived in such a remote region seemed beyond reason.

The town consisted of two occupied buildings, a bright green bar and a faded yellow church. Men hung around outside the first, and a few women went in and out the second. Small, nearly naked children appeared outside our windows selling rocks—not any special kinds of rocks either. Just plain old rocks. Hect gave them each a coin from the gas change, which made them happy.

Just as the Commander told us, the Rio Grande fanned out wide and shallow atop a solid rock bed. We drove through the slow-moving current and, once on the other side, traveled on real asphalt through Big Bend National Park. Massive mountains surrounded us, along with canyons, cliffs, and wide-open ranges of desert flowers—but not for long. The land flattened out as soon as we left the park. On a two-lane highway to Marathon, Texas, I felt as if I were back home finally, although not really.

The feeling was more like being Hect's prisoner transported through familiar territory.

We headed west on Highway 90 through hills of boulders broiled purple by an unrelenting sun and, just at twilight, intersected with Highway 80 at Van Horn. The town, judging by the way it'd been built on either side of the two-lane road, existed because of travelers heading either east to Dallas or west to El Paso. On both sides of the asphalt, a long stretch of curio shops, diners, motels, auto mechanic garages, five-and-dime stores, and gas stations went from one end to the other. When we arrived at the "X" spot marked on the map, I did a double take. A neon sign outside the dump of a motel had an unusual name, to say the least.

    HOBOS
    AND
    BUMS
    MOTEL

Other than wandering drifters, hitchhikers, and tramps, the place didn't seem like one that would attract many travelers, certainly not vacationing families. Once we got close enough to read the sign in the half-light before dark, however, the name made better sense. Part of the neon bulbs had burned out, concealing the name of the rundown place.

    HOBOSTEIN
    AND
    BUMSTEAD
    MOTEL

Hect drove past the front office and parked in front of room number five. A naked light bulb outside the door attracted a swarm of flying bugs. At about eye level, a fist-size crater in the wooden plank caused Hect and me to exchange worried looks. He motioned to knock. After returning a glare to let him know how I felt about his being "the boss" all the time, I went ahead and tapped lightly.

A huff and a moan came from behind the door. Hect motioned again, this time rolling his hand, which I took to mean knock harder. I did.

Something leaned against the door, shoving it shut tighter. "What?" a muffled voice called.

Despite the Commander's warning, I almost answered when Hect shoved me. What a close call that'd been. I took a deep breath and tapped on the door a third time.

"Ye'th? Who i'th it?"

Did that ever give me pause. I stared at Hect, who looked back just as wide-eyed. Neither of us knew what to think.

"Who'th knocking, I th'aid?" the voice asked louder. "Who'th out there?"

Neither one of us had blinked so far, at least I hadn't. How was it possible to tell if the person behind the door had a lisp or else disguised his voice on purpose?

"Th'ay th'omething out there. Who i'th it?"

Questions flooded my mind. Had we come to the right address? Was this the same motel marked on the map? Did we stop in front of room number five for sure? I felt the number plate on the door. It seemed securely attached—not a loose "two" that swung around upside-down.

"Th'peak up, I th-said!" the voice barked, growing irritated. "Who'th knocking out there? Th'ay th'omething, th'upid."

If I'd bothered to imagine what Acey Elu sounded like, it sure would never have been anything like what I just heard. Some scary maniac. He sounded more like a kid talking while sucking his thumb.

Just to make sure, I stepped back and recounted the rooms from one end of the building, then counted again from the other end to double check. Sure enough.

"Th'ay!" the voice shouted from behind the door. "An'ther out there. Why'd you knock and then not th'ay nothing?"

Come to think of it, who wouldn't feel sympathy for the man? A normal person would want to know who knocked on his door at this hour in a pigsty like this, much less an escapee on the run from the law. Hect put a finger to his lips, evidently sensing my resolve weakening, and motioned for another knock.

Before my knuckles hit the wood, the door swung open with such force Hect and I both teetered with the inward rush of air. The man before us had shoulder-length ringlets of hair. A scar divided his forehead in half from his hairline to the bridge of his nose as if an axe had been buried there, but his most striking feature was a pair of wide, roving eyes that looked past us as if searching somewhere far beyond.

"Who'th there, I th'aid?" he asked softly, sounding as if talking to himself.

A chill ran from the back of my head to my heels. The man moved his head this way and that, rising on his toes now and then, until I wanted to duck down out of his way, but dared not move. Though we stood directly in front of him, it seemed we could walk away and he'd never know we'd been there. Frankly, I would've liked nothing better.

"Th-peak up, I th-aid. Who i'th it?"

Every fiber of my being wanted to answer him. It went against my grain not to say something. A more awkward situation I couldn't imagine. Could he not see us? Was he blind? If so, why did he keep searching, trying to find who knows what.

"Who i'th out there? Come on, talk to me. Who are you?"

Hect elbowed me, no doubt as a warning to keep quiet, but the unexpected touch startled me. I flinched. My jerk went unnoticed, though, as the man continued to stare past us eerily.

How long could this standoff keep up? Someone had to make the first move. For one thing, the bugs from the light bulb had flown inside and were now dipsy-doddling the ceiling light. The room would soon be full of them.

Regardless of the Commander's warning, someone had to speak up or we could be standing here all night. What other choice was there? One of us must take charge. Just as I started to introduce myself, the man whirled and stalked back into the motel room.

Now was our chance to make a run for it. I grabbed Hect's arm, but he shrugged me off. Before I could make another try, the man returned hugging a wrinkled grocery sack, evidently his belongings. He bowled between us as clean as a seven-ten split, his locks bouncing on his shoulders, and climbed through the ambulance's two back doors. Noises inside the wagon indicated he'd settled into the jump seat in back of the passenger side. If things weren't bad enough, the nutcase ended up directly behind me.

"Th'tart up you," he demanded from inside. "Th'hove it in gear and let-th go."

That brought a question to mind, but not about to speak out loud in case the man in the ambulance was watching, I decided to use ventriloquism. "Who's he talking to?"

Hect murmured something unintelligible.

"What?" Even though I'd asked without moving my lips, I leaned in close enough to hear his answer. "Say again?"

"Uh-un," he muttered. "The motor maybe?"

CHAPTER 15

A Border Guard

THE COMMANDER'S INSTRUCTIONS HAD BEEN to retrace the same route on our return trip that we'd taken to pick up Acey Elu, but that proved easier said than done. It'd been daylight on the drive to Van Horn, but we returned in pitch-black darkness. Road signs that on the way had been clearly readable and turnoffs that had been visible for a quarter mile or more went by as if traveling in a tunnel. Unable to see past our own headlights, which mainly reflected what looked like the bodiless eyes of deer along the shoulders of the road, I worried we'd been heading south too long. I couldn't prove we'd gone past our turnoff, though, until we passed a reflective highway sign that curled my toes and made me grit my teeth.

Presidio, Texas
Pop. 7,359

Our speed slowed as Hect must have seen the sign also. Now what? Even if we had enough light to read the map, the city limits sign showed we'd missed our turnoff long ago. Arriving at Presidio, the sister city of Ojinaga, Mexico, meant we'd taken the very route that Ju had forbidden us to take. A Border Patrol inspection station lay dead ahead. The ambulance rolled to the shoulder and stopped.

Hect's quandary was obvious. What to do now? Should we keep going or turn back? If we kept on, we'd meet the inspection station, but if we turned back, no telling where the turnoff might be, and we could run out of gas. The constant mumbling coming from the back seat quieted all at once.

"Th'ay!" Acey Elu piped up. "Why'd we th'top?"

Neither of us answered. To hear a clear voice after the murmuring the whole trip unnerved me, to say the least. The ensuing silence rang in my ears.

"I th'aid," the man growled, "why're we th'topping?"

What could we do? Not only had we been commanded not to answer, but who knew what or who the weirdo might be talking to—the motor, who? If only he'd say a name or in some way let us know who he meant.

"Thi'th i'th my final warning," he snarled. "Th'omebody better th'peak up. I'm not kidding either. You don't want me to th'ay it again, believe me."

Quick-thinking as ever, Hect put the jeep into reverse and drove back until the headlights shined on that sign beside the road.

"*Per'th'dio!*" the man gasped. "Well, I'll be hanged. I didn't th'ee the th'ign going by. Boy howdy, thi'th place bring'th back a fond memory or two."

I never felt such relief. The oddball's attitude had changed completely. For the first time he sounded almost pleasant.

"My old boyhood home, Ojinaga," he mused. "I hadn't been back here th'ince I dropped out of grade th'chool and moved to Chicago. What a good time I had. Running barefoot all over the place, having rock fight'th with other kid'th, dunking their head'th underwater in the river until they near drowned. Man, what fun that wa'th."

Despite my having no idea who he might be talking to, his reminiscing about his childhood made him sound normal for the first time, like a regular guy. Had I misjudged him? So what if he mumbled to himself? Who doesn't act strange now and then? Maybe his problem was that he didn't have a friend. What if I made an effort? A friend might change his whole personality. Who knew?

"Okay, th'tart up and get back on the road," he said at last. "I can't wait to th'ee my old hometown again. Let'th go."

Our troubles weren't over yet, not by a long shot. Straight ahead an inspection station with armed border guards awaited us, but on the other hand, a U-turn would almost certainly throw our temperamental rider into a tantrum. I debated in my mind what our next move should be.

"Th'hut up!" Acey Elu shrieked in an ear piercing yell, his foul mood reviving. "Th'ilence all of you!"

Startled by the sudden outburst, I jerked so my knees bumped the dashboard. What happened? Everything was going along so well. What caused his shout? Had he read my mind? Could he hear my thoughts?

"Who invited that bunch of loud-mouth'th in here," he kept on angrily. "I'd like to know who. I want quiet, not a bunch of yick-yakking critter'th. Th'o th'hove off, all you varmit'th!"

So that's it. He'd meant the desert sounds—coyotes yelping in the distance, the sleepy "cooo-coo-coooo" of a hoot owl, nearby crickets creaking. To muffle the noise, I eased a hand over and rolled up the glass. Maybe he wasn't such a regular guy, after all.

"And good riddance! Now get thi'th thing on the road. Move it! I'm in a hurry."

Hect accelerated. What other choice did he have? I felt sorry for my used-to-be best friend, regardless of how he acted. He had to know what trouble lay ahead, but how to help him shoulder the responsibility without talking?

Once we entered the outskirts of Presidio, Hect veered off the main highway onto a side road. His intent was obvious. An upcoming intersection at an overpass meant he had decided to turn around and head back the way we came. This would almost certainly end in disaster. Even if by some miracle Acey Elu didn't notice we'd changed directions, we'd either run out of gas eventually or get even more lost. But how to warn him? Left with no choice, I decided to break my silence when a stroke of luck prevented it.

As we came underneath a streetlamp that lit up the intersection, a scruffy-looking hitchhiker leaped from the curb and made a run at us. He looked wild-eyed and desperate, like he'd been waiting for a ride a long time. The vagrant held a piece of cardboard in his hands, waving it wildly. Hect swerved to miss him, and the hand-scrawled sign splat onto our windshield before flying off.

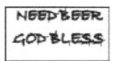

Other than looking like a hermit out of the desert, the tramp appeared harmless enough. He had on what looked like a bathrobe with a rope for a belt. A small, mangy dog accompanied him, barking at his heels.

"Hit him!" Acey Elu screamed so loud I ducked my head into my shoulders. "Hit the religiou'th nut! Run him down!"

With no place to stop, Hect went ahead with the turn and reentered the highway we'd been on, headed back the way we came.

"Mi'th'ed him! Go back! Turn around! How dare we mi'th the Bible-thumper!

For the life of me, I couldn't figure out what triggered the man's outrage. Did he hate hobos? Or small dogs? Or had he been offended the tramp asked for beer money? What was it?

"Go back, I th'ay!" the loon lisped. "Don't ignore me! No wacky reverend can wave a religiou'th th'gn in my face and get away with it."

So that's it. The sign or rather the message. He'd been insulted by what had been written on it—not about the beer, the "god Bless" part. He really *was* off his rocker. If such a harmless wish could throw him into such a violent temper, then our going back the way we came could cause an even worse fit of rage. Left with no alternative, I reached below the seatback and tugged at Hect's shirt. He slowed down, having gotten my signal evidently, and made a U-turn. We headed back toward downtown. Thankfully the sign-waving hitchhiker had moved on.

"If I ever th'ee that holy Joe again, I'll th'how him a thing or two. He can't force hi'th religion on me. I won't allow it. He'll think twice before he trie'th to convert me."

We avoided one calamity, but an even bigger one lay up ahead. Enough blinking red lights covered the international bridge to look like a train wreck. And yet, I still faced the same dilemma. If I attempted an escape, Hect would try and stop me, not to mention Acey Elu, but if I returned to camp, Centipede would be waiting. There had to be a third option, but what? One possibility would be to cause such a ruckus at the bridge that all three of us would be arrested. If I did that, though, Hect would become my sworn enemy for life. He'd blame me for losing the only family he ever had, not to mention ruining his one chance to amount to something. I couldn't do that. Besides, I still hoped he'd change his mind and go back to being the same old Hect so we could be best pals again. For now then, I'd just have to play along.

One look at the long lines headed into Mexico and anyone could tell it had to be either Friday or Saturday night. That was one thing in our favor. Overwhelmed with the volume of traffic crossing over, the Border Patrol guards wouldn't have time to motion many into the inspection stations. Sure enough, closer in, the inspection bays had waiting lines behind cars with their hoods and trunks open and luggage scattered around.

Our lane inched ahead steadily. With bumper-to-bumper traffic on one side and barricades on the other, we were hemmed in. Many cars contained young people leaning out the windows, calling to one another, laughing, and girls squealing. Now and then the doors flew open and kids swapped riders around. Brother, did I ever feel left out and blue watching all the carefree fun.

As we neared the entry into Mexico with both lines rolling at a slow but constant pace, I noticed a chubby border guard holding a clipboard standing to the side of our lane. After a quick word with each car occupant, he waved them through. Everything seemed to be going normally, but not for long.

The realization hit like a Mack truck—*a quick word!* That 'quick word' with each carload happened to be passengers declaring their citizenship. Why hadn't I thought of it before? On weekend shopping trips across the border with my parents, everyone had to state their nationality before crossing, but how could we now? How to say "American" without our lunatic passenger overhearing? Added to that, there was no telling what the nutcase might say when his turn came, if anything. Oh, what to do? I couldn't decide. If only we'd stop and let me think, but no such luck. Our car rolled to the front seemingly twice as fast as before—three cars left, two cars, one car, and it was our turn. I rolled my window down with a sick feeling.

The border guard leaned over, took a step toward our car, glanced to the back seat and then to the front, as he'd no doubt done a thousand times tonight. Dressed in a green uniform with a red stripe down his outside pant leg, he looked under the car body briefly.

"Nationality?" the man asked.

No one answered.

He held up a hand to stop our roll. "Nationality?" he repeated, still appearing preoccupied.

No answer.

He looked up. His expression changed. A frown drew down bushy eyebrows over a nose the size of a gourd that spread his eyes wide apart. "State your nationality, folks?"

Just as all seemed lost, an idea occurred to me. The situation could actually turn out to the good. This might be a chance to get rid of our irritable passenger. If I got the guard's attention off us in front and onto the grumbler in back then, assuming Acey Elu refused to state his nationality, he'd be arrested and we could declare ours and drive on. Once I got Hect alone, he was bound to listen to reason and forget all this idiocy and take me home. My idea might be a long shot, but it seemed worth a try.

I caught the guard's eye and jerked my thumb toward the back seat. The official bent that direction, cocked his head over, but then returned to me. "Can't make out a word the old gent's saying." He wiped his nose on the back of his hand, which mashed over on one cheek and snapped back. He leaned the other way again. "What's that? Eh? What's that you say?" He came back to me. "For all I know, the gent's singing the Star-Spangled Banner, but he's got to speak up so I can hear."

This time I drew a circle around my ear with my finger in the universal sign for crazy.

"Oh, now I get it." The guard smiled. "Talking to pink elephants, is he? I seen lots such gents tonight, but now being soused won't do for an excuse. He's got to voice his citizenship, tipsy or otherwise. If he don't, I'll detain him."

I barely kept from bouncing up and down. A home run! I grinned big and nodded with all my might, but the official's big nose got in the way, floating in between us like a pitted moon.

"Oh, well," the man said, "let's give the old gent a sec to gather up his wits. We'll get back to him. You boys go ahead and state your nationalities."

Crestfallen, it occurred to me that this was the problem with government workers these days—no one sticks to the rules. However, left with no choice, I did the only thing I could think of and nodded my head.

"Nope, won't do," the guard sighed, showing signs of exasperation. "Regulations state you must verbally voice your citizenship unless physically incapable. No dashboard-doll declarations allowed. Now I got cars behind this vehicle stacked clear past Amarillo. Either you two announce your nationality, or I'll detain the lot of you."

That finished us as far as I was concerned. Just as I gripped the door handle, ready to step out, Hect leaned in front of me, twiddling his fingers. For a second, I thought he'd lost his marbles too, until he motioned for the guard's clipboard. Then everything made sense. He wrote one word across the sheet of paper.

"'American!'" the guard read, taking his clipboard back. "Good enough. Sorry for your troubles, young'un. Got a nephew who ain't been able to speak since birth, and it's a mighty tough row to hoe too. Now young'un number two, what about you?"

I doubted the guard would've gone for both of us being unable to speak, but the exchange gave me time to think. When all else failed, there was always the old standby. Even though I hadn't practiced in ages, it was my last hope. I faced the guard straight on, snatched the pencil out of his hand and clapped it between my teeth, and without moving lips, sang: "Land of the free and home of the brave, the good old US of A."

"Wha...?" The border guard looked to his left and right, then back at me. A grin spread, causing dimples in both cheeks. "Shoot-fire, sonny, how in the name of Moses did you do that? Why, I'd'a swore someone spoke next to me. Gave me a real buzz, you did."

I couldn't have been more pleased and gave him back his pencil.

"Yes, siree, that was a heckuva trick—a heckuva trick," he said, wiping his nose along his forearm. "I'd give anything to see more, but I got a line behind you longer than a mobster's funeral. I must admit, though, you boys give me a bigger kick than any group tonight. Just for that, I'll let the old gent pass."

That knocked me backward. I couldn't believe it. Not all of us. I hadn't meant for my performance to be *that* good.

"Before you go," he said, casting a glance behind us at the waiting cars. "If you boys are headed below Ojinaga, you'd best get your pap a pitcher of coffee. Highway 16 is thick with Federales, and they ain't nice guys, like me. They won't be none too tolerant of your not answering them. Word is they're on the prowl for antigovernment types, so take my advice and go on a route off the main road." He rubbed his nose on his shoulder. "Now pass on."

After crossing the bridge, we broke away from the traffic and turned onto a dark residential street. I knew what Hect was thinking. Where to now? We may have bluffed our way past the border guard, but the same wouldn't work with the Mexican army. Plus, the Commander's map was useless in the dark. From all appearances, we'd be stuck here until daylight.

Hect parked. Houses without lights lined one side of the street except for here and there a window glowed dimly with a flickering lantern or candle. Across the road, a black wall hid a vast desert with stars outlining the tops of invisible mountains. Thankfully, the desert sounds had quieted, so I left my window down.

"Why'd we th'top?" Acey Elu asked. "Get going. I'm in a hurry."

I wanted to ask to where? On what road? Not back on the main highway that led to the Mexican army, so which way? This street, once the houses ended, would run out, and then there'd be nothing but endless sand.

"What're we waiting for?" Acey Elu repeated irritably. "Let'th go, I th'aid. Go!"

Hect started driving, but I couldn't take it anymore. After the road ended, we'd make it a ways, perhaps even a long ways, but once the hard-packed ground gave way, we'd end up buried to our hubcaps. I'd been stranded with no water in the desert once, not again. No matter what. I braced my hands on the dashboard in case a hard kick came against my seat back, like the Commander warned. As much as I hated to be the one to speak up, somebody had to. Who else would? "Go—*where?*"

CHAPTER 16
Breaking the Silence

THE LONGER THE SILENCE CONTINUED, the more the tension inside the cab increased. Outside the ambulance window, our tires sizzled on the paved road with the intensity of an incoming artillery shell. A low cough came from the back jump seat. After a phlegm-clearing gargle, Acey Elu hemmed and hawed as if uncertain how to begin.

"Who th'aid that?" he whispered at last, sounding cautious.

No answer.

After my rash outburst, my nerve failed. What came over me? Why'd I have to open my big mouth? Now that I'd thrown caution to the wind, I didn't know what to do. Should I remain silent and hope the lunatic forgot what he heard or else maybe think he imagined the voice? Or, should I try and talk my way out of it? Come to think of it, Acey Elu might be glad to have a non-imaginary person to talk to. Maybe, but maybe not.

"Th'omeone th'aid th'omething, who wa'th it?" he asked, his voice lifting in volume, sounding more confident. "Th'peak up!"

The blood pounded in my ears until I had no idea how no one else heard it. What to do? Should I wait him out, or speak up? He might forget, but how long should I wait? Oh, why'd I give in to such a reckless, foolish impulse? If only we could go back in time to before I'd spoken. I'd never say another word.

"An'th'wer me!" he barked, growing louder. "I heard whoever th'aid 'Go where?' Th'ay it again."

The quiet dragged on as the dark outside the windows seemed to close in on us.

"You better th'peak up, I'm warning you! And real th'oon, too. I'm getting madder by the th'econd."

The tension was such the skin seemed to be shrinking on my skull. Could this be the start of one of his tantrums? Maybe I should answer, after all. Was there a chance of charming the maniac? Perhaps one of my old gags out of the Joke Shop? Something like the hand puppet that worked so well at the mess hall table at camp?

"Thi'th i'th your final warning, whoever you are. Out with it, right now! Th'peak up!"

As I busily sorted in my mind through different sketch ideas, a presence came up close behind my head. Each puff of breath tickled the hairs on the back of my neck. It felt like some wild animal was sniffing me while I played dead. The only thing that kept me from opening the door and diving through it was the thought of winding up lost in the desert at night again.

"Wa'th it you?" he murmured, his breath hot against my ear. "Did you th'peak a th'econd ago?"

I didn't have a chance to answer. A hand clamped onto my neck as strong fingers drilled into tender nerves. My head flexed backward and my mouth opened in a soundless yell.

"Th'peak up! Th'peak up, you! Wa'th it you?"

Left with no choice as gristle crackled in my neck, I couldn't take it any longer. "Agggh! Meeee!"

"I thought th'o. You th'poke, didn't you?"

"Meeee! Meeee! I did!"

"There, that'th better." He sounded calmer, but didn't let up on his grip. "What a relief. For a th'econd there, I thought I wa'th hearing voice'th. Who are you anyhow? Come on, out with it." He gave me a shake. "Before I th'queeze th'o hard your brain'th ooze out your earhole." He tightened his grip. "Come on."

"Tim! Meeee..." Pain filled my head. "...I'm Timmmm!"

"Well, fancy that. A Tim, huh? And Tim can talk, too. Here I thought you wa'th unable. How come you didn't th'ay nothing at the motel, Tim?" He relaxed his grip.

With the release of pressure, my head felt like it would float away. Colored specks wandered before my eyes, and I felt on the verge of fainting. "I, ughmmm…"

"You heard me. Why didn't you tell me who you wa'th? How come the whole time I kept talking, you gawked at me like a th'ick vulture? Are you rude? Didn't your mother teach you any better?"

"Well…" I couldn't think.

"Here we could've been chatting away the whole trip. With no one to talk to, I've been babbling to my own th'elf for company. And then, watching how our driver dealt with that border guard, I wa'th th'ure neither of you could talk."

"No." I cleared my throat and swiveled my neck around, working the kinks out. "I can talk."

"It'th one more example of how American parent'th don't teach manner'th. Back when I wa'th a kid, if I ignored a grownup like you two did, my dad would knock me on the head hard enough to leave a pumpknot. Why, you two are no more than a couple of th'poiled brat'th."

"If I can only explain." Thankfully, I regained my faculties somewhat. "We were told not to talk to you."

"By who?"

"The camp commander. It's the truth, word of honor."

"Why would he th'ay a thing like that?"

I started to repeat the story the Commander told about the driver who got impaled on the steering column, but thought better of it. "He worried we'd offend you."

"I *am* offended. You near-about gave me heart failure a th'econd ago. When you th'poke, I feared I heard a th'pirit."

I wasn't sure I heard right. "A what?"

"Th'pirit. A th'pirit. You know, th'upernatural."

"A spirit?" Had he meant what I thought he had? "You mean, one that actually talks?"

"Certainly! Don't you know nothing? A th'pirit can talk. And when they do, you better pay attention. If you don't, they do awful th'tuff—haunt you, bring trouble, even make you feel puny and without any th'punk. Don't you know that?"

"Oh, sure, sure—a *spirit*." Despite the odd conversation, my only hope was to keep the weirdo talking and try to make a connection, but he mustn't be made to feel peculiar. To get him to relax, he must be made to think I discussed such things all the time. "Now I got you. Too bad you didn't say so before."

"I did."

"Naturally. I see now, yes, that's all perfectly normal. There's nothing wrong with talking to, well, as you say, a spirit. People ought to talk to whoever they please, whether to spirits, ghosts, goblins, leprechauns, whatever. And don't get me wrong, I'm familiar with such things myself, yes, very familiar." Despite my rattling on with whatever came to mind, I felt the beginnings of a relationship. If only I could keep him talking. "To tell the truth, I know quite a bit about, well, spirits. Once I went to church in Mexico and to a Christian concert in Albuquerque, New—"

"I hate church," he interrupted, his tone lowering. "And more than anything, I hate the do-gooder'th who go there. I do all I can to fight religion."

Talk about a blunder. Here I'd gone and offended the man. He sounded madder than ever. I promised myself not to do that again.

"All a preacher today can talk about i'th th'in." He snorted. "Th'in! Phooey!"

As bad as I hated to ask for a repeat, he'd lost me. "Sorry, but all a preacher today can talk about is *what*?"

"Th'in, th'in. You know, *th'in*."

"Oh, yes, I see." I didn't at all, but rather than ask him to say it again and take a chance on further irritating him, I took a guess. "You're right. I couldn't agree with you more. I'm sick to death of all the talk about losing weight. Is that all anyone thinks about these days, women especially? I hope to never hear another word about dieting."

"Dieting?" he said. "What dieting? Oh, now I get it. No, not 'thin' like th'kinny—*th'in* like wrong behavior. You know, a th'inner." He didn't say anything for a moment. "Th'ay, are you mocking me?"

I cringed inside. Another blunder. I seemed to be full of forehead-slappers. I'd done the very thing I vowed not to do. "Mock You?" Now to try and repair the damage. "Oh, no, I'd never mock you, honest! I—I'm just not thinking straight these days, is all. To tell the truth, I have a bad habit of not paying attention and then failing to hear what people say. My mother claimed it was my worst fault."

"Well, pay attention to thi'th. Anyone make'th fun of my th'peech defect won't live to do it twice."

"Yes, of course." The near-disastrous exchange made up my mind. Forget making a connection with the daffy fellow. He was too easily set off. The best strategy seemed to be to finish this subject as soon as possible. Just as I was looking for a way to gracefully end anymore topics, Acey Elu slapped Hect on the shoulder.

"I got to go, driver. Th'top here. Turn off the motor and give me the key'th."

Hect did as told. Acey Elu snatched the wad of keys out of his hand and the rear doors opened noisily. "You two th'tay put. I'll be back." The doors slammed and the sound of his talking to himself grew fainter.

I waited a moment before saying anything. "Where's he going, Hect?"

"Who knows? Ain't able to see nothing in the dark."

"Is he leaving?"

"No."

"What's he doing?"

"Guess"

"Oh." I was taking a risk by talking but couldn't help it. "I wish he would leave."

"He ain't…I mean, he's not."

"Yeah, but I wish he would. What'll we do, Hect?"

"Quiet. I hear him."

Sure enough, his muttering returned just before the back doors opened and then shut again. The car body tilted under the man's weight. "Th'tep on it. Let'th drive."

I hoped Hect would say something and give me a break, but instead we drove on in silence. With all his other changes, my once best friend had turned into a man of few words. As we bounced around inside the cab driving through the black formless desert, I couldn't stand the suspense. Any moment we could run off the edge of an unseen gulley or plunge headlong into a cactus patch or ram a sand dune and get stuck. I needed some answers from our lunatic passenger, and fast. "Can I please ask where we're going?"

"Not far," Acey Elu muttered. "In the morning, we're off to Juarez."

That floored me. Juarez had to be a good two-hundred-plus miles due west. Even worse, from what I recalled of the Commander's map, there'd been no lines that showed any road from here to there. I had no intention of ending up lost out in the middle of nowhere again. Something had to be done. "What about the mountains?"

"Th'imple. We'll go over or around them."

"In this old ambulance?"

"We're in a limo compared to what I've made the trip in. Try going in a broken-down old wagon. I've done it more time'th than I can count. When I ran away from Chicago, I came back to Ojinaga to hide from the draft board, and lived with my grandpa. He bought Candelilla wax up and down the river and, once he got a full load, he'd deliver it to a factory over the border from Juarez. He did pretty well, too."

"What kind of wax?"

"Candelilla. It come'th from a plant about two feet high. Farmer'th grow it, cut it, boil it in a pit, and the wax float'th on top. They cover fruit with it to keep it from rotting, and for lip balm, chewing gum, even paint. You've been eating Candelilla on fruit all the time and hadn't known it."

"You mean, there's an actual road that goes along the Rio Grande?"

"Not Rio Grande. Over here it'th Rio Bravo. And I wouldn't call it a road, but it can be driven. You have to detour inland for a mountain here and there, but th'o what."

"Rio Bravo? Why do they call it that?"

"On account of only the foolhardy go near it, or crazy."

I didn't care to be either one. "Where to after Juarez?"

"You tell me. You two know the way from there. Or, you better."

"To camp, you mean."

"That'th why you two came for me, right? When I got word you wa'th coming, they told me you'd driven from Juarez to camp before, th'o I made up my mind to take the long way around. Few people know about the river route and the one'th who do, won't take it. Too much danger. No one would think we'd go that way. Are you afraid?"

"No." I wasn't about to tell the truth. "Who knows, it might be fun."

"Ye'th, fun." He cackled. "And it get'th even funner at a hairpin turn on a cliff a half mile above the Rio Bravo. You let one wheel go off the edge and over you tumble clear down to the water. We leave at daylight."

I didn't know which I dreaded more, traveling the treacherous road or spending the night confined with the madman. How could I possibly sleep with him around?

"There!" Acey Elu hollered. "Up ahead. We'll th'leep there."

Of all the surprises, a tiny cluster of lights glittered on the dark horizon. Only a little brighter than the stars, the sparkling jewel-like bunch indicated a structure of some sort. By now, feeling somewhat more comfortable talking with the man, I had to ask. "What is that place?"

"You'll th'ee."

CHAPTER 17
Murder

~⁀

NOW THAT ACEY ELU AND I were on speaking terms, he became the exact opposite of the Commander's warning. He acted so glad to have a real flesh-and-blood audience for a change that he wouldn't shut up. It wasn't long before I wished for a return of the time when he talked only to himself.

He told of growing up in these parts, of how after "gramps ate his last taco" and they'd buried him, he'd taken over the delivery business; how he'd fallen in with a gang who were more interested in hanging around the bars in El Comedor, Los Fresnos, Barrio Alto, and San Augustin than in dealing with the farmers along the way. By the time they got to Juarez, the produce had all been swapped for tequila. One rainy day, he'd driven the wagon off into a swollen river during a flash flood, losing mules, business, and all.

Along with his many other quirks, Acey Elu added one more to the mix in that he kept demanding Hect stop in the middle of nowhere, then out the rear doors he'd dash. Either he had an overly small bladder or else an oversized complex about needing to go. Whichever, he went through the same rigmarole each time of having Hect turn off the motor, take out the key ring, hand them over, and then repeated the same threat not to "th'tep out'th'ide for nothing," but he needn't have. Where could we escape to? Besides being in the middle of the desert, after all the twists and turns so far, who knew where we'd ended up? The only things visible at night were the far-off rectangles of lights.

Closer in, the lights became lampposts with hooded spots surrounding a large, metal building. I'd seen nothing like it in Mexico. Such a modern warehouse out here away from prying eyes had to be up to no good, but what could it be? The expensive structure, along with the bright lights, stood out like a Fourth of July fireworks display. Hect stopped at a tall chain-link fence and a man stepped into our headlights amid a haze of dust.

"Key'th!" Acey Elu ordered, reaching over the seat and snatching the wad from Hect's hand. "Don't you th'tep out'th'ide for nothing." The man slammed the rear doors with such force my ears popped. Both men began talking within the headlight beams.

Hect leaned over the steering wheel, squinting. "It's him," he said so softly he could have been talking to himself.

"Who?"

"No one."

"Aw, come on, Hect. Tell me. Who is it?"

"He's the one kept asking me all them…er, *those* questions before I left. Bum-Eye, I call him."

I bent forward, studying the man closer. "Yeah, that's the guy with the white eye. He helped me at the mess hall before my fight at the water tow—"

"Curious type, Bum-Eye is," Hect interrupted. "Asked all sorts of stuff—where I was headed, who was going along, when I'd leave, such as that. Why so nosy, I wonder."

"Maybe just being frien—"

"So I asked the other guys about him."

He'd talked right over me like I hadn't said a word.

"They knew him," he kept on. "Bum-Eye had been prying around them too, so I reported him. He'll regret it when those camp security guys catch up to him."

Why bother talking after that? What was the use? He didn't listen anyway.

The meeting between the men finished. Acey Elu waved at us. After driving into the gate, we entered the building. Talk about a surprise. Instead of containing smuggled stuff in the way of guns or drugs like I figured, we'd entered an office supply warehouse. From one wall to the other there were desks, file cabinets, swivel chairs, typewriters, and all sorts of workplace equipment, enough to outfit offices from here to kingdom come. A short way past the entrance, Acey Elu stopped. "You two th'leep here."

I looked around for a bed. "On what?"

"Your back'th'ide, for all I care. And don't either of you touch that furniture. It'th brand new and about to be exported. I don't want any of it damaged. Not one th'cratch. Don't even think about getting comfy by tilting back a th'wivel chair and propping your feet up."

I started to ask for a blanket and pillow, but decided against it.

Acey Elu left. Just before the door shut, the warehouse lights went out except for one security bulb on the back wall. I scuffed my foot on the gritty floor. "How're we to sleep on cement?"

Instead of answering, Hect walked off into the shadows.

The idea of being left alone gave me the willies. "Are you coming back?"

No answer.

"Hey, Hect!" I couldn't stand the silence. "What's all this, you suppose?"

"Office stuff." His voice came out of the dark.

"I can see that." At least he'd answered. That was something. "But for who?"

"You'll see," he said from somewhere. "Maybe yours, if you don't get anymore dumb ideas about running away. It's meant for graduates to set up their offices. If I read and study real hard, a few pieces might end up in my own place one day."

If that didn't beat all—Hect caring about reading and studying. Who'd he become anyway? What happened to my fun-loving best pal? Saddest of all, I didn't much care for the new version.

I came upon a stack of boxes piled against the wall beneath the one security light. They contained bundles of papers that, when held up to the light, appeared to be official-looking documents, most in foreign languages. I'd seen similar ones in doctor offices and on the walls of principals at school. From what I could tell, they were diplomas, awards, and certificates from organizations. The curious part, though, was that none of the spaces for names or dates had been filled in. But then, at least they'd do to keep us from sleeping on cement.

Hect did even better as he found newspapers. These would work for something to cover up with as the building had already cooled off from the chilly desert air outside. It felt safest to sleep under the security light and I began layering certificates for a mattress. Hect did likewise. Our beds wouldn't be soft by any means, but they'd keep us off the dirty floor.

After the documents had been stacked an inch or so off the cement, Hect spread his newspapers messily while I arranged mine. First, I tucked a bottom sheet under the edges of the stacked documents, making a tight bundle; next, I arranged newspaper on top of my mattress and slid under the pages, being careful not to untuck any edges. Once settled, though, I couldn't relax. "Hect, do me a favor. Cover my feet."

"I'm in bed."

"I know, but it's nothing for you to sling your papers off and back on. If I get up, I'll have to start over and remake everything."

"Too bad."

"Aw, come on, lend a hand. If my feet are out, it'll bother me, and I won't be able to sleep."

"A shame, ain't it."

Ignoring the sarcasm, I tried reasoning. "Look at it this way. If I have to get up and remake my bed, it'll disturb you even longer."

Hect threw off his covering and, grumbling under breath, pulled the papers over my feet. Once back in his own bed, the pages rattled fierce enough to let me know his heart hadn't been in it.

"Thanks, Hect. You don't know how lucky you are to be so…" I started to say "sloppy," but thought better of it. "…so unparticular."

He didn't answer.

Just before I slipped into a comfortable drowse, a noise outside the building brought me alert. "What's that?"

"Wind. Go to sleep."

"The wind wasn't blowing."

"T'is now."

The wad of newspapers under my head went flat, proving all but useless for a pillow. Unable to fluff them, I made more crumpled balls into an even bigger pile.

"Quit that durn rustling!"

"I'm trying to get comfortable."

"I'm moving."

"Okay, okay, I'll be quiet." But it wasn't easy. Something even more bothersome wouldn't let me sleep. My top sheet began acting weird. A corner of the newspaper lifted up, bent backward, fluttered for a second, and lay back down. Even though I hated to, I reached over and tapped Hect.

"What now?"

"My sheet moved."

"So?"

"By itself. Watch."

The newspaper repeated the motion, bending backward and flapping, only this time the entire page curled halfway back.

"The wind, I told you."

"In here?"

"Might be a window's open."

"There are no windows. We've got a visitor."

His answering grunt meant he was sticking to his "wind" theory.

"We better go see. Just to make sure."

Hect groaned.

"Come on."

Even though we tried being quiet, getting out of newspaper beds was like scooting from under empty tin cans. Hect and I then ran tiptoed toward the door at the other end of the building, staying in the darker portions of shadows along the edge of the furniture. A man cleared his throat, and we froze in our tracks.

"You're imagining things," a voice said out of the blackness. "You've lost your nerve."

I recognized him—the guy who helped me in the mess hall before my fight with Centipede, the same one who'd been outside the fence. If he hadn't spoken, we would've run straight into him. As it was, we ended up almost close enough to untie his shoelaces.

"I'm not, you know...I'm not imagining things," a second voice said, this one unfamiliar. "And I, um, resent your, you know, insinuation."

Although I couldn't identify him, judging by his hurried tone and pauses, he sounded jumpy and distracted.

"In a situation like ours, you know,..." the unfamiliar man paused. "Did you hear anything just now?"

"No."

"I thought I did."

"It's nothing."

"Okay. Anyhow, like I was saying, in a situation like ours we've no time to waste. We must leave now while there's still a chance to...to...you know, to get away. No cause is worth dying for."

"Calm down. Now you're getting me edgy," the one from the mess hall insisted. "Get a grip."

"I am, you know, calm. Don't keep saying that. Now listen, Acey is onto us, but even if he only mistrusts us, he's not about to take any chances. Anyone who crosses him dies, period. He wants control of the movement, and he'll let nothing stop him."

"Control—you can't be serious. Acey Elu is mad as a hatter."

"That's what, you know...That's what everyone thinks—that he had a...a...oh, you know, a nervous breakdown, but he didn't. US authorities were tipped off where to nab him. The leadership wanted to get him out of the way because they thought him too unstable, but now they discovered their mistake. They need him for donations. So they want him back, but as a figurehead, only he's not about to be any figurehead. He wants control. Anyone who, you know, stands in his way is a target. He's eliminated plenty in his time. Two more, like us, would mean nothing to him."

"Take it easy! Why do you think I risked our meeting like this? Because if you don't relax, you'll blow our cover, if you haven't already. Now I spoke with him tonight and assured him we're as reliable as anyone. Acey doesn't suspect a thing, as far as I can read him, but one look at you, and he'll know whose side we're really on."

That perked me up. Had I heard right? Whatever side Acey Elu was on, these two were on a different one. So who were they? Spies maybe, but for who? A government? Which one? Then again, what did it matter? At this point, an enemy of my enemy is my friend, as the saying goes. Maybe they'd be willing to help us. The next question was, should we step out and reveal ourselves? If only I knew.

"Now look," the nervous-sounding one continued, "I'm just as much a pro as, you know, as you are. But I've learned some things you haven't. For instance, I heard from a trusted source that Acey Elu is planning an attack on the camp. Maybe it's a coup d'état, but it's our duty to escape and issue a warning. That's why I'm upset. It has nothing to do with, you know, with me losing my nerve."

"It happens to us all at one time or another," the one from the mess hall persisted. "That's why we have colleagues. It's policy to send two so, if one loses control, the other can step in."

"*Lose control!*" he gasped. "That's the biggest pile of, you know, pile of garbage I ever heard. What gave you that idea?"

"Because whenever you get rattled you start saying 'you know' until no one can tell what the blue blazes you're talking about. I'm sure Acey Elu has noticed. He might be crazy, but he's not stupid."

"Okay, maybe I am a little uptight, but that nutcase is a cold-blooded savage and no amount of assurances from you will appease him either. He might talk to himself, but he's as sly as, you k—as they come. I say we make a run for it now."

At last I was convinced they could be allies, but my problems weren't over yet. How best to make contact with them? Should I stand up? No, if they had weapons, they might shoot first and ask later. Should I then call to them from behind a crate? No, they might run away. If only I could talk to Hect maybe together we'd come up with an idea. Then again, he hadn't been in a very cooperative mood lately.

A loud BANG echoed in the dark, sending my heart into my throat.

A second, lesser bang sent a bell-like ringing throughout the building. It took a moment to realize the source. A metal door must have swung open and crashed into a wall, but why? Had it blown open? Had someone entered? A light breeze passed along the floor.

From the opposite end of the building, a single ray of light pierced the dark. The beam swept the warehouse's interior from side to side, finally settling on the two men, both with their mouths wide open. The men staggered backward from the spotlight, their faces stricken and drawn. If the beam had strayed off the two, Hect and I would've been exposed.

"No!" the man from the mess hall cried, his hands up.

"Him!" the other one howled, pointing at the first guy. "Not me! It was, you know, *him*! He's the one who, you kno—"

A spitting noise cut him short. A second squirt of flame flickered from that end of the building. Three more followed, each one ending in a muffled "shunt!" as the men in the spotlight contorted, craned backward, shuddered, and jerked. Instead of crying out, the men made sizzling noises like spittle rushing through clenched teeth. The pair drifted down the wall, one body settling atop the other. As the shooter approached, the beam of light enclosing the two shrank to an ever tighter circle until Acey Elu stood over them. An odor of burned gunpowder arrived. The flashlight shined on the grisly scene, where the two murdered men lay in a heap with limbs tangled, both staring out half-closed eyes.

"Wake up, you two!" Acey Elu shouted. "I th'ay, wake up! I mean it!"

Now I'd seen everything. Just as it seemed the killer couldn't get any crazier, he pulls a stunt like recalling them to life. Then it struck me he might not be talking to his victims. I turned to find Hect already gone.

"Hey, you two!" the killer called. "Where are you? Get up. We're leaving."

I scampered on all fours back the way we'd come, staying in the darker shadows. Once at our beds, I found a quaking form underneath a cover of rattling print. A light beam swept around the building.

If given a choice, I would've gotten under the newspapers, too, and pulled them over my head, but what good would that do? Instead, I stood fully erect and stretched as if just waking up and edged over into the ray of light.

"Here we are! At this end!"

I nudged Hect with my foot. "To your feet!" I'd spoken without moving my lips as the spot of light shined on my face, blinding me. "Act like you just woke up." I put all the urgency I could muster into each word. "It's our only chance."

Hect stood beside me in the beam of light, shielding his eyes. The only sound was knees rattling inside jeans, but I couldn't tell if they belonged to him or me.

"I told you two to th'leep here," Acey Elu snapped. "Why'd you go down there?"

"N-Newspapers!" I breathed a word of thanks for whatever premonition inspired me to move. "We found them to sleep on."

"Next time you do like I th'ay. Come on. Get the lead out."

His last remark, considering what I'd just witnessed, made my insides quake.

CHAPTER 18

A Spirit Speaks

MY OPINION OF ACEY ELU had changed. Before tonight, he'd seemed different and misguided, definitely odd, at times out-and-out weird, but then again, he probably had a bad childhood; his dad might've been too harsh or his mom too mean, whatever. Now I saw him as plain old evil. As far as him having an unhappy childhood, who cared? He wound up vicious, that's all. Anyone who could take a life and casually go about his business without so mu…A memory stopped me. Had there not been a time when I'd done the same thing? What about when Hect and I thought we'd burned up that hobo in the shack? Anyone looking at us would have thought we'd "gone about our business," too. So, what's the difference? Not so much, maybe. Ours had been an accident, while Acey Elu's had been intentional, but the outcome would've been the same. Who's to say he's bad and we're not? All in all, then, maybe there wasn't a lot of difference between us, only opportunity.

We left the warehouse in the ambulance before first light and, with Acey Elu in his jump seat in back directing the way, took a dirt road down to the "Rio Bravo." From there, we headed northwest away from a rising sun, following a two-rut trail that ran next to brown, moving waters.

Now and then, we traveled through fertile valleys where the river rounded a bend and earlier floods had left a delta. These offered a welcome break from an otherwise long stretch of rocky, salt-cedar-choked sandbanks. The road cut inland to circle the mountains but then met up with the wide river again.

By noon, we reached an actual graded road at the tiny village of El Provenir. A roadside stand sold tamales, plus bottles of soda called Jarritos that tasted sweeter than a handful of sugar with a fruit juice chaser. We filled the jeep's tank with the last of our gas cans but kept the empty ones in case we came across another station.

Back on the road, a sight across the river brought a groan from all three of us. An orange cloud the size of the Red Planet took up half of an otherwise blue sky. The dust storm appeared stationary, but anyone who knew the desert recognized that before long gale-force winds would hit, along with barely breathable air and blinding dirt, turning a clear day into a gritty, half-lit twilight.

At the town of Praxedis G. Guerrero, we turned inland away from the sandstorm, but by Ciudad de Guadalupe hurricane-force winds hit. The sun shrank and dimmed until no brighter than a tan disk. Surrounding mountains faded to outlines. Dirt obscured the road ahead in fast-moving brown tides.

At another of his frequent stops, Acey Elu hurried out the rear double doors into the roaring wind to the other side of a small bluff. A single sage bush atop the mound whipped back and forth. For a paranoid killer, at least he was discreet.

"Hect?" I kept my eyes fastened on the tiny hill as the wind shredded the sandy top. "We've got to get rid of him."

"What's that mean?"

"He's killed two already. We're next."

"Why ain't he done it 'fore now?"

"We're useful, that's why. We know the way to camp from Juarez. He doesn't. Once we get someplace he recognizes, we won't last long, believe me."

"You maybe got'a point, fact'ta'the'matter."

That made me turn away from the mound. "You sound different."

"How so?"

"Different, you know. Like you used to be. What's up?"

"Them two back there was my fault. It was me who turned in Bum-Eye and got them both kilt. At camp they told me one day I'd amount to some'n, be upstanding, a respected member of society. They didn't say nothing 'bout being a party to a killin'."

My hopes sprang to life. Did this mean we were back to being friends again? Was my best buddy back? "So, you no longer believe all that baloney they taught at camp?"

"Not baloney neither," he said firmly. "And I still believe 'cause it's true. I'm just tired of puttin' on airs, 'specially for the likes of you. Too much trouble."

My spirits sank again. "What you're saying is, nothing's changed—about us, I mean?"

"That's 'bout the size'a it."

"Yeah, well, so much for that." I looked back to the mound. "At the moment, you and I got bigger troubles. We're witnesses to what happened at the warehouse, whether he thinks we saw it or not. Once we're no longer useful to him, he'll have to get rid of us for good. By then, it'll be too late to do anything. We've got to make our move now."

"I ain't escaping, I already told you. Neither are you. And forget doing nothing to disappoint the Commander, 'cause we're completing this mission."

"Look, we're in over our heads. This isn't about escaping or failing to complete our mission; it's about staying alive. It's either Acey Elu or us."

"How you know for sure?"

"Didn't you hear him after Presidio? You and I are the only ones who know the way from Juarez to camp. As soon as he figures the route, it's good-bye, Charlie."

"Yeah, maybe."

"No maybe about it. Those two at the warehouse said before they died that Acey Elu had plans to retake control of the movement. And how could he do that? Alone? Not likely. He must have a small army somewhere waiting to help him as soon as he gives the word. He'll for sure kill us and maybe a lot more, even the Commander, who knows?"

"You're guessing."

"And you're not thinking. It all adds up, I tell you. Acey Elu plans on taking over everything and everyone. Which do you think the Commander would appreciate for us to do the most—complete this mission or prevent a possible overthrow of the camp?"

"Yeah, I s'pect maybe. But even if you're right, what can we do?"

"Get rid of Acey Elu."

"How?"

"I've been thinking about it ever since we left the warehouse." I risked a glance to see how he took the idea so far. No resistance. "I think I know a way to control him, but I need a distraction."

"A what?" he asked, sounding suspicious.

"Some way to throw him off. A prop. A misdirection of some sort."

"Misdir..." He groaned. "Don't tell me you mean that stuff about throwing your voice you're always talking about."

"Right, but I need a way to get his attention off me." I was talking to myself as much as anyone. "Something like Pepe, my hand puppet, or a stick in my mouth, but it has to work while sleeping. Then I can be a voice out of the blue, so to speak."

"What in tarnation...? You better start making sense, and fast."

"There's no time to explain. He'll be back any second. I need a prop, I tell you. Come on, think! What could convince a person that someone was so sound asleep that there'd be no way of connecting them to a voice? Something that'd get the attention off me completely."

"Not snoring, for sure" he snorted. "When you get'ta gruntin'n'rumblin' like a pond of toads, everyone within hearing knows it."

He hadn't meant it as serious, but the idea gave me pause just the same. "Snoring, huh?"

"Forget it," he said dismissively. "Anyhow, why're you asking?"

"He's crazy, isn't he? He hears voices, doesn't he?"

Hect gulped out loud. "Don't look now, here he comes."

"Okay, when I—

"Shush! He's outside your door. Don't—"

The roar of a mufflerless motor drowned Hect out, along with a series of loud backfire *pops*. I stole a peek in time to see a rusty old truck pass by with a load of kids huddled on the flat bed without sides. Acey Elu yelled something, which delighted the riders on back, who laughed and stuck out their tongues. The madman shrieked louder.

I shut my eyes and eased my head over against the window frame, while wishing we hadn't wasted so much time arguing. Now there was no chance to give details. I'd just have to tell Hect what to do and hope he didn't mess up. "When you hear a voice, act like you don't, especially if he asks you." I spoke without moving my lips in case the madman might be watching. "Whatever happens, play dumb."

"That shouldn't be hard, in your opinion."

"Don't start." This was no time for a petty argument. "Just remember, if he asks if you hear anything, say no. *No!* Got it?"

"I hope you know what you're doing," Hect whispered.

"I don't, but we have to try something."

He whimpered softly. "I got a mighty bad feeling."

At the same instant he spoke, the rear doors opened. Dust coursed through the car's interior, and particles whirled up from the back floorboard, settling on my arms. I didn't brush them off. The jeep rocked side to side.

"Bad feeling?" Acey Elu repeated. "Th'o you can talk like your buddy here, huh? Neither one of you got a lick of manner'th. You got a 'bad feeling' about what?"

In the silence that followed, I sensed Hect's hesitancy. Up until now, he'd let me do all the talking and was no doubt finding it not so easy to make small talk with a full-blown maniac.

"Hey! Did you hear me, driver? By the way, what're you called."

"Hect," he murmured.

"Hect, huh. What a th'tupid name. Anyway, Hect, I don't like being ignored. Now, I'll repeat what I th'aid and you better th'peak up. 'Bad feeling' about what?"

"Nothing."

I peeked out one eye. Hect glanced at me with a pleading look, but what could I do?

"Nothing, phooey! I heard you th'ay 'bad feeling' a th'econd ago. You hadn't talked the whole trip, th'o why now all of a th'udden? Who were you talking to?"

Hect hacked a fake cough. A stall, obviously. Even if I could find some way to help him, what was there to say? Acey Elu had him dead to rights.

"Me, I guess," Hect said finally. "Talking to myself. I seen Tim yonder sawing logs in no shape to drive so I says to myse'f, 'I got a bad feeling,' about my chances to get him to rest me a spell."

"Wake the lazy th'ucker up."

"Naw, that's okay. He hadn't slept in days. He'd fall asleep at the wheel anyhow. Once he conks out, nothing wakes him up. Let him sleep."

"No wonder you don't talk," Acey Elu commented. "From that accent, you th'ound backwood'th ignorant. I wouldn't th'ay nothing either."

I had to admire my onetime friend's ingenuity. Not bad, not bad at all. He'd given a pretty solid alibi on the spur of the moment.

"Well, you're out of luck, dummy," the madman continued. "Don't expect me to chauffeur you two around like th'ome underling. I'm the VIP here, and don't you forget it. Keep driving, like it or not, and th'top griping."

For the next few miles, no one spoke. Strong winds moaned outside as the sand pelted the ambulance in a grainy static. Acey Elu began noisily rattling newspaper he'd brought from the warehouse, reading in a low murmur. Other than that, the only sound came from Hect, who hummed under his breath nervously.

I breathed in a slow, measured rhythm, snoring lightly, now and then slurping my lips together as people do when asleep, but in reality I'd never been so keyed up. Unsure how my idea would work, much less if Acey Elu would fall for it, I knew the dangers of trying something new without practicing first. No one I'd heard of had attempted what I planned, but then again, maybe that wasn't all bad. If no one had heard of throwing your voice while at the same time snoring, wouldn't that mean there'd be less of a chance of anyone thinking it possible? Whatever, I had no other ideas. While inhaling, I snored a little louder than normal, but then exhaled, ending a low sigh with a moaned, "Aaace Cee Elll-youuu."

The newspaper popped in back and the murmured reading stopped. Hect's humming accelerated.

Not having practiced ventriloquism lately, I'd been uncertain how well my voice would carry, but to my ear at least, the words arose from in back of the ambulance. No one spoke. Acey Elu rumpled his newspaper. Other than that, all remained quiet except for the humming. The madman's mumbled reading began again.

In any performance, timing is crucial. Back in the days when I used to practice in front of a Joke Shop audience, I tried different lengths of pauses to see which produced the best effect. Not too long, not too short, just right. "Aaace Cee Elll-youuu."

The newspaper popped again.

Hect's humming accelerated, approaching bumblebee speed.

I rolled my head to give Acey Elu a better view, hoping the madman would get a good look at my unmoving lips. Plus, with my chin tucked into my shoulder, I could talk out the corner of my mouth. I kept my breathing at the same rate—a softly snoring inhale, followed by a shorter exhale, ending with a sighed, "Aaace Cee Elll-youuu."

The newspaper crumpled. "Quit that th'upid humming, Hect! How'm I to think with you buzzing like a baboon. Did you hear anything?"

"Like what?"

"Like th'omeone talking. A voice?"

"Yours?"

"Not mine, halfwit. Th'ome other one?"

"Who?"

"One more th'mart crack and I'll put a kink in your neck that you'll never get untangled. Now did you hear a voice a th'econd ago, or not?"

"The wind, maybe," Hect said. "This jalopy's got more gaps than Granny Lilly's smile. What you heard was a whistle, I bet."

I didn't appreciate the attempt. Here I was trying to be convincing as a 'spirit' and he's pawning me off as the wind.

"Don't tell me what I heard," Acey Elu returned. "I heard a voice, no air leak."

"But there's only us."

"You're ignorant of the th'upernatural, I can tell. A clod like you from back in the boondock'th wouldn't know about paranormal th'tuff."

"Pair'a *what*?"

"Para-normal. You've never heard of it, have you? It'th the hidden world. There are force'th all around that people know very little about, unlike me."

"You don't say. My-my. Sounds mighty interesting."

It struck me that Hect had taken my place in trying to keep the weirdo talking.

"Oh, it i'th!" The lunatic's voice enlivened. "I could teach you a lot. I'm pretty much an expert on th'uch thing'th."

"It's all news to me."

"I didn't know about it either to begin with." His voice took on such an eagerness like I hadn't heard the whole trip. "One night when I wa'th a kid, I couldn't th'leep for fear of lightning and thunder. A'th I lay there all atremble, I heard a voice that told me not to worry. I felt calm for a change. I had company. We ended up talking until dawn. From then on, we chatted every night. He became a real pal, my only pal, and let me tell you, after a day of my old man yelling and boxing my ears, I looked forward to a kind word. We'd laugh and have th'uch a good time at night that I'd hate to get up in the morning."

"Really." Hect sounded hesitant, but who could blame him? Their conversation could've come straight out of a booby hatch. "You two got to know each other real good then, I s'pect."

"Like an older brother," the man sighed with a note of longing. "But one day he went away. No telling what became of my old pal. I've interviewed every witch, warlock, and medium I could find trying to get back in touch with him, but no luck. I'd do nearly anything to find him again."

As much as I hated to break into their off-the-wall conversation, it was getting us nowhere. As far as I knew, our lives were at stake. As soon as Acey Elu didn't need us anymore, we were goners. For a moment back there, I almost had him believing in the 'Voice.' I sensed it. A little bit longer and he might really have been hooked, but then Hect butted in and everything went haywire. It was time to push ahead and hope for the best, but first I had to put the lunatic at ease with the so called 'Spirit.' This wouldn't be easy because, in order for my idea to work, he'd have to get comfortable enough to trust me, or 'it,' but I never remembered being so nervous. Nevertheless, at the end of a snore and following sigh, I moaned, "Aceceeee Elll-youuu, I thee by the thou—"

I broke off midsentence. It'd been the biggest blunder yet. I meant to say "I *see* by the *sound* of your voice you doubt," hoping that'd reassure him, but instead I accidently mimicked the madman's lisp. It'd not only been a colossal flub, but one that was impossible to fix. He already thought I made fun of him once, now here I'd done it for real.

"You again!" the madman gasped.

What could I say? I was trapped.

"I thought you'd gone?"

Words failed me.

"And what'th with the 'thee' and 'thou' talk? You th'ound like you're out of old-timey England. Who are you anyhow, King Th'oloman?" He snickered.

I had to think fast. Any hesitation now and all would be lost. One good thing, at least the delusional madman answered me, or 'it.' Now what? I'd never actually had a part in a Shakespeare play, but I'd helped set the scenery often enough and watched my share of performances during my community theatre days. How hard could it be? I snored on the intake of air, then sighed, ending with, "Nay."

"'Nay,' you th'ay?" he snorted with a half-laugh. "Not him, huh? Then who *praytell*?" He added the last mockingly.

After another light snore, I moaned, "King Arthur."

"King Art—well, I'll be dipped!" the madman groped. "If that don't take the cake. You mean, that 'thee' and 'thou' th'tuff i'th for real?"

"'Twas the manner in my day." Hardly missing a beat, I had no choice but to grab a breath, snore and press on. "The age of chivalry."

"A long, long time ago, I bet?"

"Aye. One thousand four score and ten." I nearly ran out of air on that one.

"Back then folk'th talked real grand all right," he admitted. "Only trouble, today I got no more idea what you're talking about than bean dip. Too bad, King Albert."

I quietly scolded myself. Would I never get this right? Here I'd fallen into the trap of amateurs—overacting. Even worse, my voice had weakened with straining, which only would get worse. After snoring, I moaned. "Authur."

"Yeah, yeah, whoever." From his tone, he was far from convinced.

Fearing things would soon fall completely apart, I had to hurry. After a snore, I groaned, "For thou, I wilt modernize."

"Modernize all you like, but I'm thinking you're a fraud. Full of hot air. Only a fool would fall for every th'pirit that come'th along. Too many counterfeit'th. *Fifteenth century*—that'th a little farfetched. You'll have to prove you're the real McCoy. Ironclad, evidence, i'th what I demand. Right now, though, I got to make a th'top. Hey, driver," he called to Hect. "Pull over and hand me the key'th."

Hect angled the ambulance to the side of the road and parked. Acey Elu hurried out the back doors as a gust of dirty wind blew in, swirling like a mini dust devil. The rear doors slammed.

"He's gone," Hect sighed under his breath. "I seen close shaves a'fore, but that one left no hide."

Still pretending to sleep, I blew a long sigh. "Whew! That didn't go well, did it?"

"Not hardly. Don't move. He's behind a bush, but he's watching."

"I'm boxed in, Hect. I don't know what to say. I've talked myself into a corner."

"Aw, a genius like you, now how could that be?"

"Save the sarcasm. I'm stuck." Except for our being watched, I would've curled a lip at him. "I'm trapped. Tell me how to get out of this?"

"What in the name of Sam Hill was you thinking in the first place?"

"How was I to know he'd doubt the existence of a voice out of thin air? It never entered my mind someone that nutty would question anything. It'd be like calling the long-distance operator a liar after she tells you the number. Who thinks like that? Now what can I say?"

"You're the one with all the bright ideas, ain't you?"

"Cut the criticism. We've no time. When he gets back, he's going to want hard proof the *spirit* is real. What can I say to convince him?"

Hect didn't answer.

"How can you leave me stranded like this?"

"I'm thinking, I'm thinking." The silence hung heavy. "Okay! Got it. It's a little un-reg'lar, maybe, but here goes. The dungeon."

"Dun...*What?*"

"Tell him you—or not *you*, but the spook—knows where his long-lost buddy is. In the slammer. Gullible as that scatterbrain is, he's liable to fall for it."

"Have you lost your mind? What are you talking about? What dungeon?"

"This here's the road me and Becca took to the movie-set prison. The joint's as creepy a place as you'll ever see. We drive right by it. When we get near, I'll clear my throat, and you can point and say that's it—the dungeon."

"I can throw my voice, not my arm. What do you mean 'point'?"

"Forget pointing then, but you can tell him that's where they got the spirit-pal he knew as a kid locked up in a cage. He'll see the place and maybe believe you."

"You're either joking, or you've gone even more bonkers than him."

"You got a better idear? He said he didn't know what happened to his boyhood spirit-pal, didn't he? And they was best buddies, wasn't they? Well then, tell him, that's what become of him. He's in that dungeon that

I'm talking about, and he sent you—or not you, but the spook—to tell him so he'll quit worrying. There's your proof."

"Is that the best you got?"

"You asked my opinion, and I give it. That's that."

"Besides being the dumbest idea ever, so what? It proves nothing."

"Says you. It *does* prove some'n, too. It's what he can see with his own two eyes. That's what he wants, ain't it? Hard cold proof."

"No one, not even someone so out of touch with reality as that loon, would ever fall for such a sap-headed, silly, ridic—"

"Shhtt! Here he comes! He's here!"

CHAPTER 19
A Spirit Dungeon

THE TWO BACK DOORS OF the ambulance opened, filling the interior with a swirl of suffocating dust. Acey Elu climbed in and took his seat. As we accelerated and gravel crunched under the tires, I stole a one-eyed peek out the front windshield. Sand swept over the highway so thick that, just like in west Texas, dirt would block the road like sandbars in a river.

No one had spoken so far. Because of it, I hoped the earlier conversation with the "spirit" had been forgotten. It'd suit me just fine if no one said anything. I resolved to leave Acey Elu alone from now on, but no such luck. The deranged killer cleared his throat, and I felt it coming.

"Let'th th'ee, King Albert, where wa'th we?"

I grimaced. Whatever possessed me to ask Hect for advice? Now I couldn't think of anything but his harebrained idea. The notion of a dungeon wouldn't allow another thought. What should I do? Stay quiet or speak? Voices in the night come and go, don't they? At least the madman said as much. Why not this one? Like his boyhood pal, this *spirit* could vanish into thin air.

"I'm waiting," Acey Elu growled. "And I'm not a patient man. Th'peak up and real th'oon or I'm liable to throw a fit."

Why'd I ever listen to Hect? By now, I would've thought of something reasonable instead of his loopy "bright idea." Oh, why couldn't I think?

"I *th'aid*, 'I'm waiting!' Where are you? Nothing get'th me more riled than being ignored. Th'peak up!"

149

What other choice was there? He would soon blow his stack anyway. How much worse could I make it? After a snore and a reluctant sigh, I moaned, "Here, Aaaa-cee Elyouuu."

"There you are," he said, calming. "Okay, a'th I remember, you were about to convince me you're the real thing. I'm waiting on pin'th and needle'th, a'th they th'ay. What'th your proof?"

If only a sensible idea would come at the last second, but none did. Having no choice, I shut my eyes tighter, snored, and sighed, "Thy childhood chum."

There came a quick intake of breath. Whatever the surprised reaction meant was anybody's guess. "Th'ay what? You know about him? You know where he i'th? I'th that your proof?"

I snored. "Aye"

"Well, out with it! Th'peak up! Where i'th he? Tell me!"

Another snore. "Thy friend is in...in..." I couldn't get it out. Hect's idea sounded so wacky at that moment, so foolish, that no one, not even someone who ought to be in a padded cell in a straitjacket would fall for it.

For the first time the whole trip, Acey Elu seemed at a loss for words. The silence went on until I thought it'd never end.

"Well? Th'ay it!" he barked at last. "What are you waiting for? Th'peak up! I'm about to blow up? Tell me where he i'th! Th'how your proof!'"

Despite feeling as absurd as ever in my life, I had to get it out. I snored, while at the same time wondering if that might not be for the last time, sighed, and moaned, "...a dungeon."

"I don't believe it."

What a fool I'd been. Only an imbecile would have listened to Hect? From the start, I knew the idea was ridiculous. What made me think it'd work in the first place?

"That old thief."

My breath caught. Had I heard right? Could it be? The shock was such I forgot all about snoring. "Beggest thy pardon?"

"I th'aid, that old thief."

"Thou art not surprised?"

"Not a bit."

"I thoughtest thou would be." Since he didn't seem to miss the snoring, I decided to give it up.

"There never wa'th a pro filcher yet who could quit the light-fingered work altogether," the madman said. "What'd they put the old bandit in the brig for?"

What choice did I have? "As thou indicated, pilfering."

"Once a thief, alway'th a thief, like they th'ay."

Curious, I had to ask. "Thou knewest him well?"

"Oh, th'ure. He taught me all kind of th'tuff—telepathy, predicting the future, clairvoyance, communicating with the dead, mind reading, but above all, reincarnation. He had lived in a new body often. During the Roman Empire, he robbed temple after temple; during the French Revolution, he pillaged cathedral'th; he even picked the pocket of Napoleon; and during World War I he made a living a'th a grave robber. Th'nitching wa'th in hi'th blood."

Up until then, it never occurred to me that the voice from his childhood had been anything other than imaginary, but a child couldn't invent such things. Then where had the ideas come from? If not out of a boyish fantasy, what had the voice been? The idea was unsettling to say the least.

Hect cleared his throat, interrupting my thoughts. I assumed his gargle to be our prearranged signal. I stole a peek. Wind-driven dust obscured the passing desert so that the blurred landscape went by in brownish forms. Had Hect's gargle been unintentional or on purpose? My only option was to trust to instincts. "There, Aaa-ceee Elll-youu."

"Th'ay what?"

"Thy childhood friend."

"Huh?"

"The dungeon." My voice crackled, but I couldn't clear my throat as that would show where the sound came from. "Out there."

"Where?"

"*There!*" It wouldn't be long before I went completely hoarse and unable to throw my voice at all. "'Tis the dungeon."

There came a stirring noise in back. "I th'ee only blowing dirt."

That gave me pause. Had I jumped the gun? Or else, had we passed the dungeon already? Too late to back out now, I had no choice but to press on. "Lookest thou harder."

"You mean to tell me the dungeon can be th'een with the naked eye? How can that be?"

The facts were getting more entangled the longer we went. I had to somehow get this over with, but how? What would explain his being able to see into the spirit world? Should I claim a miracle happened? A sudden yelp startled me.

"I th'ee it, I th'ee it! Well, I'll be... Of all the..."

Such a feeling of relief overcame me I wanted to shout along with him.

"Holy cow, look at that, would you? Who would've thought th'omething that big would be out here in the middle of nowhere? Don't the place look wretched, though? A more bleak dump I've never th'een."

Hect slowed the ambulance to a crawl, and I couldn't help sneaking a peek. The prison appeared dreary as a castle in a brown fog. Amid the blowing dust, stone blocks the size of coffins made up a towering wall. Ivy climbed halfway on the outside, giving the place an old-timey look, but since such vines could not exist in a bone-dry desert, the setting had an otherworldly aspect. At each end of the wall, unmoving men stood with rifles in the windows of the guard towers.

"Th'top the car!" Acey Elu demanded. "Park it, I th'ay!"

Hect obeyed and pulled over.

"My dear old chum," he groaned sadly in a rare show of emotion. "I hate it for you, poor old wayward kleptomaniac."

Just as I worried he might start bawling, a hand clamped onto my shoulder, stopping my heartbeat cold.

"Hey! Wake up, you! Jump alive!"

I sat up, waving my arms and gasping for breath. The sudden fright left me tingling all over.

"Th'top the engine, driver. I don't want any interference. That'th better. Here, face me, you. Wake up!"

I turned, fighting off the urge to leap out the door and run. The man's dark-circled eyes made him look like he'd been through a long illness. His breath smelled sickly.

"Quit that th'tupid blinking. Look at me! Look at me, I th'aid!"

I could hardly think.

"Don't you turn away or even think about it." He gazed around, his eyes rolling, looking for who knows what.

The quiet that followed intensified unbearably.

"How come I don't hear a voice now?"Acey Elu asked quietly. "Where'd it go, I wonder?"

The lengthening hush continued, growing weightier by the second.

"No, not a th'ound. Only th'ilence, dead th'ilence. How odd."

I swallowed, feeling my Adam's apple lift and fall in a mushy gulp. No one I'd ever heard of or read about had ever performed this close to an audience. The prospect terrified me. Could this be done? Had any of the best, including Edgar Bergen or The Great Lester, ever attempted such a feat? Doubtful, very doubtful. If I pulled this off, wouldn't that put me up there among the greatest of all time?

"Hello!" the madman called, looking toward the back of the ambulance where the voice had been coming from. "Hey! Cat got your tongue? Th'tage fright, maybe?"

I pretended to yawn, partially covering my mouth with my hand. "O, Aaa-ceee Elll-youuu, thou doubter."

CHAPTER 20
Dead Man'th Pokey

∿

THE DUNGEON SAT AT THE end of a dirt road. Two large wooden gates stood between us and the movie set that, judging by their recent construction, had been built by the film company. One gate blocked the entrance from the highway and attached to the property owner's spaghetti-slung wire fence. The other one had a sentry booth and anchored an iron-pipe fence surrounding the movie set.

"Drive on," Acey Elu commanded, aiming a finger in between Hect and me. "Go on, drive on!"

"Drive on?" Hect gasped.

I well understood his quandary. The gates looked sturdy, and we had practically no front end to protect us from the impact.

"Don't doubt me! Go through them! Now, drive on."

Hect still didn't accelerate the ambulance. "Won't we crash?"

Though I shared my onetime friend's hesitancy in ramming the first gate, he was taking a grave risk arguing with the killer.

"Go! Now! Hit the gate! Hit it, I th'ay!"

On closer inspection, I saw what the madman meant. The gates were balanced on pivot posts and weighted to remain closed. To open them, a metal plate on the bottom had to be bumped. Anyone could see the trick lay in hitting the barricade with the right speed. Too slow and the gate wouldn't open far enough to pass through, but too fast would spin the heavy object around before anyone entering could clear the opening.

"Go! Go! Go!" the deranged man railed, losing control. "Now! Now!"

Understandably cautious, Hect gave it the gas too timidly. The ambulance struck the first gate, sending it lumbering out to the break-over point, wide enough to drive into the opening, but then the barricade lost momentum. The gate shut on the front quarter panel, tearing off the driver's mirror and the door handle, then clawing the rear quarter panel and finally ripping off the back bumper, which lay in the road.

"Harder. Harder, I th'ay!" the madman shrieked. "Go! Go!"

Hect overdid it at the second gate, slamming the bumper plate with such force that the heavy barricade spun around and crashed into us, denting in the inside, knocking out both rear door glasses, and almost tipping us over. A garbled cry arose from in back.

With the ambulance still drivable, remarkably, we kept going at a limping hop from what must have been a bent back wheel. Hect parked next to the prison wall that rose high above us. No one spoke for a long moment.

The dungeon looked spooky enough without the blowing dirt. Such an empty, awful solitude hung about the place that I half expected some undead ghoul to walk up.

Above the main entrance, a gigantic bell hung in an arch. In Old West days, the bell must have announced arrivals and doubled as an escape alarm, but now it swung in the wind. Instead of clanging, as the housing lacked a clapper, the thing creaked in a sort of eerie rhythm. The steady eek-ing had an unpleasant effect on me. Unrealistic as it may be, the bell seemed to be clanging away in the spirit realm.

"Dead man'th pokey," Acey Elu groaned in a miserable way.

I shuddered, but a second later nearly dropped my jaw. The bell did something so extraordinary that at first it seemed impossible. As I watched, the thing actually raised up, elevating under its own power. After my initial shock, the reason became obvious. A rope attached to it passed through a pulley and fastened somewhere behind the wall. The bell edging higher could only mean that the wall had tilted forward, pushed by the high wind no doubt. Whatever anchored the base of the wall must have broken loose. Considering where we'd parked, the next powerful gust could topple the massive thing, which would land on top of us. A low moan from the back jump seat interrupted my thoughts.

"Th'omeone i'th watching."

Whoever he meant, whether the painted-on guards in the watch-tower windows or some bogeyman he'd imagined, it really didn't matter. Any second we might be beneath a pile of rubble. The bell jerked up on its own once more, reaching the pulley. Should I warn the other two? Evidently neither one had noticed. Or else, should I duck down and hope the ambulance top was stout enough to withstand the weight? Maybe we'd get lucky, and only Acey Elu would be crushed. Maybe, but maybe not.

"You two th'tay here," Acey Elu ordered. "I'll go take a look. Give me the key, and don't either of you th'tep one foot out the door."

In removing the key ring, Hect nervously dropped them and had to search around on the floorboard.

"Th'peed it up, you! I don't have all day. Hurry, I th'aid!"

This only served to rattle Hect and make his search all the clumsier.

"Th'hould either of you th'tep out the door, I'll be on you like a ton of brick'th."

His choice of words, considering what would soon collapse on top of us, couldn't have been more unnerving.

"Now hurry up with that key, you!"

Hect handed them over. As soon as the lunatic closed the back doors, I reached for my onetime friend, while keeping one eye on Acey Elu's back. "Run for it."

"Speak up."

"I can't! That's all I got." My voice barely got above a croak. "Run for it."

"Why?"

"The wall's falling."

Hect leaned close to the steering wheel, looking up. "Holy...!"

Acey Elu made it to the base of the structure. Otherwise, he might've seen what hung above him like an impending avalanche. The housing of the bell had wedged into the pulley and cocked outward like a loud-speaker, meaning the rope was the only thing keeping the wall upright. When it broke, the madman would end up with the bell for a hard hat, not to mention being buried under considerable debris.

"Hect, it'll hit us, too! We'll be crushed!"

The motor started. The revving gave me such a sudden fright that I bounced in my seat, my head brushing the headliner. "How...?"

Hect pointed to a single key in the ignition. "Taken it off the ring. Not bad, huh?"

"Not b—go, go!" I clutched the dashboard. "Go!"

We accelerated. Rocks rattled noisily in the wheel wells. The bell bounced off the hood, denting it like folding a tin can, crashed into the windshield, spider-webbing the glass, and flew off the side. A thunderous, splintering racket made me whirl in my seat in time to see the madman take one step backward before vanishing in an onrushing dust cloud. The wall had hit with the force of a giant's shoe stomping down. Barely able to see through our spider-webbed windshield, we skidded to a stop.

Once the air cleared, a heap of blocks lay piled where we'd been parked, along with twisted pipes, broken boards, and tangled strands of wire. It looked more like a demolition site than a dungeon.

"Flyswattered him!" Hect cried and tromped the accelerator.

We passed through the first gate but stopped before the second to kick out what was left of the windshield. Behind us, to my surprise, Acey Elu, instead of being buried alive, stood among the wreckage, waving a broken, wedge-shaped block the size of a grave marker. He hurled the stone away with no trouble at all. I rolled my window down, trying to make out his screams amid the howling sandstorm.

"What's he saying?" Hect asked.

"Can't hear. Sounds like the same word over and over."

"What word?"

"Quiet." I cupped my hands behind both ears. "Strange, I never heard...sounds like...Sty-something. Sty...Sty...Sty-what? Sty...ro...? Oh, *Styrofoam*. He's mad the stone blocks are fake."

Acey Elu then picked up a broken timber-size beam and began beating the ruins while bellowing at the top of his lungs.

"What's he saying now?" Hect asked.

"Can't hear because of the wind. But it's another word over and over. Sounds like...Pla'thick. Or, plath-tic. Oh, *plas-tic*. That's it! 'Plastic.'"

Acey Elu pulled himself out of the wreckage, but with his first step, the lookalike stones gave way, and he sank out of sight. He'd struggle back up on top only to vanish once more. After another attempt, he pointed his hand in our direction.

"Gun! Hect, he's got his gun!"

The ambulance leaped forward, crashing into the last swinging gate, knocking the barricade off its anchor pin and into the road. We drove over it. Whitish smoke escaped from under the bent hood, the steam hitting us in the face. The bell had either broken a hose when it hit, or else it had damaged the radiator. Hardly able to see, Hect zigzagged right and left, throwing the wet fog this way and that, giving us brief views of the road. Faint pops could be heard behind us.

Our barely drivable ambulance hobbled along amid billowing clouds while at the same time, shaking like it would fall to pieces. With no time to change to the spare tire, putting as much distance between us and the dungeon seemed more important. We hadn't gone more than a mile, though, when I noticed something that changed everything. I sat bolt upright. "Stop! Stop! Stop this thing!"

Hect slowed and pulled off the road.

"What're we thinking?" I looked at Hect through thinning steam. "We turned off wrong. Juarez's the other way." In all the commotion, I hadn't given it a thought. "We're headed back toward camp."

"So?"

"*So* a lot. We can't go back there. What'll we say?"

"The truth. What happened."

"That we failed in our mission and left Acey Elu in the desert? Oh, that'll go over great."

"Well, there ain't no going past that nutcake and give him another shot. He made it to the highway by now. Anyhow, we ain't going far either way on account 'fore long the motor will overheat. We're spewing out water as is."

I looked around and took stock of where we were. "There's a pond out there, and it's not too far."

"Out there?"

"Trust me."

His eyes narrowed. "Why should I trust the likes of you?"

I ignored the snide dig. "Remember? I told you of the tank and the windmill I fixed."

He looked off into the distance. "Best be close by."

As steam escaped from under the hood, I told him briefly about the time Victor's truck got hot and how Raul and I drove into the desert and found the pond. At the end, I couldn't help finishing with a troubling thought. "If only that rickety old windmill hasn't blown over in the high winds."

CHAPTER 21
Attack

IN THE STRONG, DUSTY WINDS, the windmill propeller spun like the contraption meant to sprout wings and take off. Algae-tinted water overflowed the brim of the tank, leaving the ground around it soupy. Hect parked the ambulance's front end close enough to the tank to splash water on the grill; then removed the radiator cap ever so slowly to prevent boiling water from erupting. To get the bent hood up, we'd used the lug nut tool for a pry bar and broken the latch. The radiator, although knocked backward, hadn't been the cause of the steaming after all—rather, a crimped water hose had a pinhole leak. By wrapping Hect's handkerchief around the hose and tying the ends in a knot, we turned the spewing into a drip.

After the engine cooled enough, we put water in the radiator and then refilled all the empty gas cans, hoping to keep up with the leak. I wanted to take a dip in the tank, but Hect said no. Whatever happened to my fun-loving friend? While Hect made repairs on the motor, I took off the bent wheel and put the spare on. We tied down the hood with a piece of wire off the windmill, and as we got ready to leave, I went ahead and jumped in the trough despite his disapproving glare. Although the quick dunk felt refreshing, the water left me smelling pretty rank.

With a good back wheel and without the steam blowing in our faces, we could drive faster now, although the sandy wind blasting in the open windshield chapped our faces raw. Worse yet, the needle on the temperature gauge climbed way faster than we expected, forcing us to stop and use our cans of water one at a time.

One thing, though, we finally outran the leading edge of the dust storm, plunging us into the clearest colors after all the brown—skies as blue as deep waters, mountains a grape purple, clouds cotton-candy white, and even the desert had the look of a golden pie crust. Thanks to my hunger, everything reminded me of food.

For the first time ever, I actually longed for a return of a sandstorm. Dirty air had a benefit I'd not considered before. The Commander had warned Hect and me when we left camp that our every move would be watched, which wouldn't have been possible a few minutes ago. Now, we could be easily seen from the mountains with binoculars, or from the air, or by someone trailing us. True or not, I had the unsettling feeling that we were not alone.

Hect stopped the car. I started to get out for our last water can when I noticed he had his chin on the hand that gripped the steering wheel, his eyes squinted as if focusing in the distance. I followed his stare.

"The air yonder," he said as one finger popped out from under his chin. "Next to that dog-eared mountain."

"You mean the one with the landslide on top so the peak folds over?"

"To the right."

"Yeah, what *is* that?"

A speck hovered in the air above the horizon. The dot, no bigger than a period, moved ever so slowly, edging in front of a foothill, finally blending in with the rocky backdrop. The way the speck vanished worried me. It reminded me of that time in the desert when the lights led me away from the gigantic tire tracks, stranding me. Hect's arm shot over the dashboard. "Yonder!"

The airborne fleck, now above the mountain, took on a familiar shape. "It's a biplane."

"Ain't no bigger than a toy."

"Commander warned us not to come this way. And here we are—in trouble again."

"That ain't the end of it." Hect nodded further to our right.

A column of dust rose off the desert floor. Cone-shaped like a whirl-wind, the base of the column moved too fast for any dust devil, but not as fast as the time Raul and I had encountered the jeep with the thugs. This cloud seemed different. Considering whatever could cross roadless country at such a clip, plus the incoming biplane, one thing became all too clear. "They're coming our way."

"I figger so. Ain't no hope'n our outrunning them in this jalopy nei-ther. We're near overheated as is."

As much as I hated to say it, what else was there? "Camp! If we beat them to it, maybe we'll get a chance to explain what happened before they arrive."

"You're forgetting one thing, ain't you? Our missing rider."

"Oh, Acey Elu, that's right." It didn't take long. "Like you said earlier, we'll tell the truth, for the most part. We got lost in the dark and our pas-senger insisted that we not turn around. They...they arrested him at the border because...because he refused to declare his nationality."

"Might work. How about the wrecked jalopy?"

"Um..." I had to think fast. "We had an accident because...because..."

"...'cause," Hect finished for me, "you couldn't hold your tongue and back-talked Acey Elu. He blowed his stack and throwed such a fit the ja-lopy went for a tumble."

Overlooking the fact of my being the blame for everything, I went ahead and nodded. "That'll have to do."

Hect stomped the pedal, and we sped away. Before long, we turned off into the Chihuahuan Desert on the same road Raul and I had taken. Once we found the giant tire ruts, or what was left after the wind finished with them, we headed southeast away from our pursuers. The ambulance stirred up such a dust ball we couldn't tell if those chasing us had gained ground. The biplane, on the other hand, now the size of my World War I Sopwith Camel I glued together as a kid, circled to the west. For whatever reasons, the biplane paralleled us instead of closing in.

Hect fought the steering wheel. Driving at such speed in loose sand threw us all over the place. Any little dip bounced us both to the ceiling.

Our handkerchief bandage either fell off or else loosened because steam escaped from under the hood, enough to partially blind us, but not as bad as before.

We crested the rise where Raul and I had taken our beating from the two sentry thugs. Below us, barely visible above a rounded dune, the top of the water tower showed we had almost made it. My sense of relief didn't last long, though, as down there my old enemy, Centipede, waited. The Commander had told us that if we completed the mission "successfully," the small-headed bully wouldn't dare take revenge, but what about now? After our failure, would I still be protected? Then again, where else was there to go?

Once we entered the outskirts of the ghost town, the biplane made a low pass over our ambulance. Shortly afterward, six armed men on horseback arrived. So that's why the dust cloud looked different—horses. One group of three riders peeled off to the right and the other group went to the left. They wore sombreros, red neck scarves, and grimy white shirts with cartridge belts crisscrossing their chests. Something told me these men were not the ones who the Commander sent to watch us. Wherever they came from, from their looks, they meant business.

After encircling the ghost town, the riders faced about their horses, then withdrew rifles from saddle scabbards. At the same time, recruits poured from trailers and scattered in all directions. I reached over and clutched Hect's shoulder. "Who are these guys?"

"Whoever, it ain't good."

What happened next might have been normal in any Central or South American country, but not sleepy Mexico. Gunfire sprayed from all directions. Barrack windows collapsed into slivers and trailer tires went flat. The sounds of sizzling whines filled the air. On the buildings, sideboards burst into splinters. A trash barrel skipped end over end down the street as dirt erupted around the tumbling object like bugs burrowing into the sand for cover.

We'd parked dead center in all of the smoke, confusion, and destruction. I hardly could think. Hect, judging by his goggling stare, felt just as helpless. Not only had we misguessed who might be after us, but we'd led them straight to camp. If we'd worried about our reception being misunderstood before, how to explain this?

The rear doors burst open. I raised my arms in surrender when, of all things, the Commander crawled in on all fours. More incredible yet, his face wore that same big grin. "Blimey, look who's returned like freeloading in-laws." He clambered breathlessly into the jump seat, occupying Acey Elu's former spot. "Marvelous timing, lads, I must say, although our transport seems a tad more bunged-up than when issued."

I forced myself to stop staring. "What is this?"

"An assault, old boy, unless I've badly misread these chaps' intent."

"By who?"

"By *whom*," he corrected. "But we will have a go on your grammar later as it's time to shove off. Press the pedal, old boy." He touched Hect's shoulder. "No sense in staying for the final act of this tragedy."

As if coming to himself, Hect jerked and swung about in his seat. As we drove, recruits ran and leaped at us, trying to hang onto the outside of the ambulance. A few managed to gain a toehold, but the first pothole sent them flying.

"Where to?" Hect cried, maneuvering among the chaos.

"Heathrow," the Commander returned. "At least our version."

An explosion beside us sent a breaker of dirt through the open windshield, pelting us with clods and rocks.

I ducked down. "They're bombing!"

"Merely one over the bow to slow our progress, I'll wager." He pointed past Hect's shoulder. "Aim to the left of that mound of vegetation."

That made me look. "Vegetation" sounded like we'd driven into a lush forest, not this barren wasteland. Sure enough, a mound of fall-colored, leafy vines lay dead ahead as big as a medium-sized hill, but the closer we got, something about the place looked suspect. Rather than rounded, the top was flat like a roof. Even odder, a strip of graded-level ground stretched away from the ivy that was bare of so much as one cactus patch, yucca plant, sage bush, or the ever-present tufts of broomweed. We drove up onto the straightaway and discovered a mesh of heavy, interlocking chain painted brown to match the desert.

Once we got around in front of the mound, a blunt nose cone like that of a rocket poked out of the vines. By then, the sleight-of-hand trick was exposed—not greenery, but camouflage netting; not a vine-covered hill, but a square hangar; and not a rocket nose cone, but a twin-engine aircraft. Out taxied a World War II Russian plane, judging by the red star behind the wings, possibly a small troop transport. The whirling props blew the camouflage netting to shreds, leaving a skeleton frame. As the plane lumbered down the runway, the Commander motioned for us to drive alongside.

Hect quickly caught up to the rolling airplane and wheeled the ambulance behind one wing amidst billows of dust, which burst through our glassless windshield, stinging our skin with the power of a sandblaster. Visibility went to zero in front, while beside us a hatch opened on the body of the plane.

"One at a time!" the Commander shouted over the roar. "Make haste. These chaps won't wait." With that, he bolted out the back doors and, while fighting through a wind-driven cloud of grime, caught up to and ran alongside the plane. Two men appeared on either side of the hatch opening and as the Commander dove for a handhold, they pulled him on board.

"Go, go!" Hect shouted. He held his shirt collar up over his eyes and took quick glances ahead. Because of it, the ambulance zigzagged all over the place. "Now!"

"What about you?" I had my shirt up, too, peeking as best I could through a buttonhole. The sand burned my hands and arms like hot sparks.

"Go!" Hect shouted, ignoring me. "Now! I can't keep up."

"Together!" Something warned me not to leave him. "Let's go."

"Get out! I can't hold this thing!"

"But...!"

"Now! You first, then me!"

I had a bad feeling, but to hesitate any longer meant neither of us would make it.

"NOW!" he swung backhanded at me. "Go!"

Left with no choice, I clambered out the back, leaped clear of the swinging doors, fought my way through swirling, blistering dust despite being almost swept off my feet two or three times. Finally I grabbed the metal edge of the hatchway, and, if not for four hands taking hold of my arms, I would have been blown away. The two men dragged me aboard. I immediately rolled over and sat up, ready to help Hect, but he wasn't there.

Behind us, the driverless ambulance, still rolling, veered off the straightaway and into a cactus patch, where it stopped. Hect, meantime, ran among torrents of sand, but the wind off the props combined with the pilot throttling down proved too much. Our speed increased as my friend got farther behind until, at last, he gave up and stood still.

"Hect!" I'd screamed with all my might. "Hurry!" I waved him on, but the effort was useless.

I looked over to my left at the Commander. "Stop! Stop the plane!"

"They won't, lad!" he shouted back through the wind, his face bunched in an out of character frown. "It's a shame. Too late."

"Slow down then! Let him catch up!" I looked back at Hect's shrinking figure. He waved, not in a desperate way, but more like to say good-bye. "We can't leave h—"

A red puff next to Hect's head stopped me. He spun a full turn around, staggered once or twice, and toppled to the ground.

"He's shot!" I could hardly believe my eyes as I watched him flop around like he was trying to get back on his feet. The biplane flew overhead of our plane, but I couldn't take my eyes off Hect, who kept on struggling. "They shot him!"

A million thoughts went through my head at once. Why? What to do? How could they? Who would help him? He needed me. How could I leave him? If the situation had been reversed, would he fly off and leave me? Could I just sit here and watch? Would my last picture of my best friend be him wallowing in the sand? As the plane's wheels lifted off the ground, I did the only thing I could think of. I jumped.

CHAPTER 22

A Wing and a Prayer

~⌐

HITTING IN SOFT SAND FROM a height of twenty feet or so, and traveling at however many miles per hour it takes to get a plane off the ground, surely above fifty, was like a rag doll thrown into a cement mixer. Arms and legs went every direction as I bounced, flew through the air, tumbled, cartwheeled, and somersaulted. It seemed I would never stop rolling. Finally slowing somewhat, I gathered every sticker burr, goat-head, cactus needle, and stray thorn along the way, coming to rest at last with legs over my head and body bent double. I feared to move in case something might be out of joint, or dislocated, or else a cracked bone might break, or a limb fall off—who knew the consequences.

At last, I got up the nerve to slowly unbend, flatten out, ease over onto my back, and rise to a sitting position. After examining my arms, legs, and ribs, while at the same time plucking out whatever had punctured me, thankfully, nothing seemed broken. Other than scrapes and cuts, everything felt intact. Evidently being as limber as a noodle had its advantages. I remembered once when Hect and I had awakened beside a pond, he said I was so covered in sand I looked "breaded for frying." That description fit now more than ever. The thought brought to mind my friend and, looking around, trying to get oriented, I spotted his figure at last, about the size of a toy soldier, lying facedown.

Beyond Hect's figure, farther in the distance, the battle at the camp continued like something out of a war movie. The biplane circled overhead of the ghost town as recruits ran every which way, and the men on horseback fired rifles. The chaotic scene jarred me out of a daze. Everything came back to me—Hect being shot, jumping from the plane— but why was I waiting? How much longer would I hesitate? Not only was Hect injured, or worse, but as soon as the fighting quit, they'd come for us.

Once on my feet, I ached at every joint, but nevertheless put one foot in front of the other. At first walking, then trotting, I managed a stumbling run back to Hect's form. Blood had splattered everywhere. Even though he lay facedown, his matted hair betrayed how much he'd bled. I could hardly bring myself to turn him over. If he'd been killed, what then? Should I stay or run to save myself? What should I do? Had I rashly jumped to my own finish? I glanced over at the battle scene going on among the trailers and the ghost town. Where was there to go?

After a bracing breath, I knelt down and rolled Hect's limp form onto his back. His nearly unrecognizable face was caked in a red, grimy paste. A gash began at the top of his forehead and ended two inches or so behind his hairline. I searched his back pocket for the handkerchief he always carried but then remembered we'd used it to repair the water hose. Reluctantly, I left him and ran to the ambulance. The front end was too deep into the cactus patch to get to the wire we'd used to tie down the hood, so I reached into the gap between the bent lid and fender. Stretching and feeling around, careful not to touch the still-idling, hot engine, I found the cloth and jerked it off the hose. Although wet and slightly greasy, it'd surely been steamed enough to be sanitized.

Back at my friend, I dabbed his wound with the wet handkerchief and cleaned his face the best I could. The gash, although long, didn't appear to be deep, but it bled worse than any cut I'd ever seen. I paused, saying a quick but earnest prayer, asking God for a miracle that the injury be no worse than a scalp wound and to please revive my friend. Hect groaned.

"Hect? You okay?"

"Hmm…"

"Are you okay?"

"Um…"

"Can you sit up?"

"Oh, man..."

With my help, he sat up.

"Here, hold your hanky against your head. Press hard."

He mumbled something that didn't make sense.

"Say again."

"Wha...wha...?"

"You've been shot, but thank God, it's only a flesh wound." I stood to my full height and dared a look toward town, mainly because the gunfire had stopped.

The biplane made a low pass over the heads of a group of T-shirted recruits, all with their arms in the air. They were being herded in front of the water tower. The riders on horseback ringed the gathering with their weapons pointed threateningly.

"Hect, can you get up?" I tried lifting him, but he was dead weight. "We have to get out of here."

"Not sure...can walk."

"Try." I lifted again, still without success. "Come on, Hect. Try at least. We can't stay here."

"Last I seen...wha' happened?"

"I couldn't leave you."

"Wasn't you on..."

"I jumped out."

"You bailed?"

Glad to see him regaining his senses, I felt relieved. "Forgot my parachute." I half chuckled.

"Ain't you got a brain?"

That stung. "I knew you wouldn't leave me."

"Don't be so sure."

I'd had enough. "Look, Hect, they fed you a line at that camp. I can't help how I was born, no more than you can. Blame 'rich guys,' as you call them, for your troubles, if you like, but before you do, ask yourself one question. Would any of your camp teachers come back for you? Or would they keep on flying, maybe at best, roll their heads and say, 'Gee whiz, isn't that a crying shame?' Personally, I think it's the last one."

Though bloodied, he looked thoughtful.

"And one more thing. Who was it who came out into the desert to tell you that you hadn't committed a crime, that there was a thousand dollars waiting for you when you got back home? Maybe you don't care about money anymore, good enough, but I bet none of your camp know-it-alls would go to the trouble."

"Yeah, s'pect." He sounded reluctant.

"Those guys spouting that rich against poor stuff might believe it— maybe, maybe not—but if what they say is right, why do they need goons like Centipede to enforce it? And why shanghai saps like us into an army to force their beliefs on others?"

"Enough, enough, I give. Maybe I have been a fool."

"More like misled, but in your place, I might've fallen for their line, too, except for one thing. It didn't jive. For instance, they taught that things would be better if they were in charge and made all the rules. Really? Why then don't they come out and tell the truth about what they want? Why trick everyone to get their way? Their whole plan is based on lies."

"Okay-okay. When you come back to find me after being back home safe, that bothered me. I couldn't figure why. And now to jump out of a plane so we could share whatever's coming, well…" He cleared his throat. "If nothing else goes right, at least you and me is back to being best buds. I hate it about treating you like I done. Sorry, pal?"

I looked away, pretending to see what was happening at the camp, but actually I needed a moment to regain control. A lump had risen in my throat, preventing me from talking. Even so, the situation at the ghost town had changed. The fighting had stopped. Worse yet, a couple of riders were headed our way at a gallop. "Hect, we've got to get out of here. They're coming."

"Where to?"

"Not the ambulance. They're bound to check there first. We'll have to hide in the desert somewhere."

"With no water, no way to stay out'a the sun. How long can we last?"

"Yeah, well…" He had me on that one. If there was anything worse than being captured by the horsemen and taken to prison, or wherever, it would be the thought of returning to the desert without water. I'd done that already and swore never to again, but the memory gave me an idea. "Hect, we've no time, so I have to talk fast." I glanced toward town. The riders, coming at a gallop, had closed the distance between us. "I told you how God saved me in the desert once. Maybe He will again. Let's pray together."

"Pray?"

"It's our only hope."

"I ain't no good at—"

"No time to argue. Now! God will help us, but not if we don't ask Him."

"But how?"

"Simple. Say, 'Jesus!' That's all! The name, 'Jesus!' That'll do it. That's all I had before, so it must be all we need. Whatever else comes to mind is okay, but it's His name that makes the difference. If you truly want Him to, no matter how hopeless the situation, He'll be there. Now, pray!"

We cried out together, but I couldn't help sneaking a peek in the direction of the ghost town. Two riders raced toward us, lying on their horses' necks, holding their rifles out at arm's length in one hand and, with the other, using the reins as whips.

A massive shadow went over the top of us, along with an earth-shaking roar. We looked up in time to see the belly of the Russian transport swoop past overhead, heading straight for the trailers and ghost town. The plane passed so low over the riders that both horses spooked, darting to the sides and spilling the two horsemen who pitched off and crash-landed. The transport then banked right and took dead aim at the biplane. I thought for a second the two would collide in midair, but instead the transport flew barely above the smaller plane, flipping it in the backwash. The biplane careened like it was caught in a whirlpool, went into a downward spiral, nicked the top of a sand mound, and made a complete forward flip before disappearing. A fireball arose from behind the hill.

Back at the ghost town, the men on horseback fired at the transport, which made a full, wide circle and came straight back. It came in so low, just missing the water tower, which toppled and burst, sending a wave of toxic black water over the recruits and the men on horses. The plane then passed over the hangar but, instead of pulling up, dropped lower yet and landed on the airstrip, bearing straight at Hect and me.

I grabbed my friend by the shirt collar and dragged him off the chain-link runway into the sand. The plane came up even with us as the back hatch opened. The Commander and the two men who'd pulled me aboard jumped out, ran toward us, scooped Hect into their arms, and carried him to the plane. I trotted along behind. One by one, we boarded. Being last in line, I ran along with the taxiing plane and jumped aboard as they picked up speed.

As we flew over the desert, I took one last look at the ghost town— the toppled water tower like a deflated ball, the men no bigger than guppies flopping around in mud, and the surrounding, rugged mountains so barren—all of it shrinking with the increasing distance. Where we were being taken, who knew? One thing, though, I hoped to never, ever, in my entire life, see this place again. Little did I know, we were headed for a place far worse.

CHAPTER 23

On the Way to...?

THE FLOORBOARD ANGLED UP AS the plane climbed. While lying on my stomach atop a grating, I stuck my fingers through the metal loops, holding on for all I was worth. After the noise and confusion, the muted drone of engines proved as disorienting as the earlier racket had been. The floorboard tilted ever steeper. As none of us could stand, Hect, the Commander, and I clung to the grating to keep from sliding down into a heap. Once the plane leveled off and we got to our feet, it took whatever handholds came within reach to hang on.

If I'd ever bothered to imagine the interior of a transport, it sure wouldn't have been anything like this. Pleated fabric covered the walls, shag carpeting went from the metal grating clear to the cockpit, and comfy sofas were positioned opposite each other. The interior looked more like a reception office of one of my dad's rich oilmen friends. The two men holding an almost unconscious Hect lay him on a couch at the back of the plane and began doctoring him. The Commander, meantime, assured me my friend would be okay, that one of the men tending to him had trained as an army medic. He then led me to the front, and indicated that I sit next to a man wearing a turban. Across from him sat a bearded man in wire-rim glasses wearing a beret. I gave the Commander a look, hoping for an alternative to sitting next to either one.

"Go on, mate. They'll not bite." He laughed. "Go ahead, get acquainted. Anyone daring enough to jump out of an airplane with no parachute shouldn't be shy about a little thing like an introduction."

I didn't move.

He bent down close. "I'll let you in on a little secret that should perk that flagging ego a mite," he whispered. "Your arrival on board with me elevated your status in the eyes of these blokes considerably. They assume you to be high up in administration. It's how I convinced them to come back for you. I told them that you two lads have top-secret priority in the movement and your loss would cripple the organization. Now then, there's no need to feel inferior. In fact, swagger a bit. Believe me, these chaps are consumed with self-importance and, not only so, but each craves to be higher up than the next, so buck up and stiffen that spine. You'll do fine. I'll take a seat in the cockpit. Go on, introduce yourselves to Acey Elu's *brothers*." He broke up at that, almost losing his balance.

The plane banked right, beginning a slow turn. The Commander, giggling away, staggered up to the cockpit. Left with no alternative, I took the seat but scooted against the padded armrest to take up as little room as possible. Unable to find my safety belt, I accidently elbowed the turbaned man, who growled. Before I could apologize, it dawned on me who he was—the one in the films at camp who had spoken under the translator.

A finger tapped my knee.

"Don't bother," the man in the beret across from me advised. He took off his wire-rim glasses and cleaned the lenses with a pocket-handkerchief. "He speaks your English, but considers it, although necessary, an inferior language, and beneath him to actually speak. Even if he did, however, he still wouldn't talk to you. I'm his assistant and even I don't qualify for small talk. By the way, where is our brother?"

"Acey Elu, you mean?" I swallowed a gulp that made me crane my neck. If only there was time to think. "So, he really *was* your brother?" I cleared my throat, stalling. "I thought it'd been a joke."

"No joke. How do you mean 'was'?"

I pretended not to hear. "The Com…" I started to say "Commander" but feared it might reduce my status in the eyes of my listener. "*Ju's* always joking, isn't he? But I'm sure you know that already."

"Oh, so you two are on a first name basis. Impressive. But, as I said, it was no joke. Acey is our brother, all right. Where is he?"

174

"Oh, ugh…Back there, I'm afraid." I pointed across the aisle in the direction of the small windows. The wisest strategy seemed to be to say no more than necessary in case his brothers shared the psycho's hair-trigger temper.

"What a pity," the bearded man sighed. "He couldn't make it to the plane, you mean?"

"No, he couldn't, in a manner of speaking."

An air pocket bounced the plane. The turbaned man next to me grumbled under his breath and gripped the armrests until his knuckles turned white.

"Don't mind him," the bearded man cautioned. "He has a lot on his mind. We all suffered a great disappointment at what happened to the camp. It was just good fortune our scouts spotted the attack and those of us who matter, made it out. Otherwise," he said, nodding at the man in the turban, "he might've been captured. You understand, he's very high up in our brotherhood."

I heaved an inward sigh. Everything made sense now. That type of "brother" seemed less intimidating than a blood relative. "It's lucky we *all* escaped."

"So true, so true," he agreed. "The attack took everyone by surprise. A spineless traitor tipped them off to our location, no doubt. It's been rumored for a long time that we've been infiltrated. Because of that, we've remained on high alert with tighter security than I've ever seen it."

This was not a subject I wanted to pursue. Our former topic seemed less likely to lead to trouble. "So, he's very high up, you say?" I glanced at the man next to me. "Clear to the top, you mean?"

"You have no idea." He rolled his eyes up toward his beret. "Only myself and a handful of others even know he exists, that's how close to the top."

"You don't mean it."

"I *do* mean it. Besides being his interpreter and adviser, I'm his personal counselor."

I thought the man's voice sounded familiar. He must've been the translator on the films at camp.

"My position," he continued, "is one of extreme significance, you understand. There's much that happens behind the scenes of a worldwide organization as ours that ordinary rabble are ignorant of." A look of alarm came into his eyes. "You may or may not be aware of that."

"Oh, of course I am!" I pretended offense. Anyone high up in an organization, as the Commander had stated he'd told everyone Hect and I were, shouldn't appear ignorant of anything.

His face under the beret relaxed visibly. "I thought as much when I saw who you came aboard with, but you can never be too careful, not knowing your position. By the way, what is your position?"

"Same as yours." I'd said it in the hopes of blending in, but judging by his gasp, my remark had been taken wrong.

"Hardly the same as *me*." The bearded man snorted. "Why, young man, you can't know half of what I do. You'll do well from here on to think first before you speak, or you run the risk of being taken for a fool."

"Really?" I could hardly back down now. Someone his equal, or close to it, would never allow himself to be high-handed like this. "You might think twice before using such a term."

"Is that so?" He paused and eyed me closely. "Allow me to ask a simple riddle, in that case, one that anyone of significance in our organization should know instantly. Tell me, if you can, our primary mission? Our methodology to achieve that goal, what is it?"

Even though I wanted to jump up and make a run for it, this was no time to act defensive. Besides, where was I to go? I had to somehow turn the tables on him, but how to do that? "Why do you ask?"

"I'm testing you, naturally."

"For what reason?" I needed to take the offensive, but how?

"To see how informed you are, why else? The amount of knowledge you possess will tell me your rank in the organization."

"But I don't know your rank."

"*Mine!*" The bearded man practically choked. "You must be joking. Either that or you're an underling of the most inferior status. I help formulate policy here. My rank is preeminent. I'm the one who'll ask the questions, and you will answer promptly, or else."

His last words gave me an idea. "I'll tell you what I do know. As you stated at the start of our conversation, there are disloyal ones among us. I just witnessed the execution of two spies at a warehouse out in the Chihuahuan Desert. Both men were leaders in high positions of trust, and both were shot because they asked too many questions."

His face lost color. "You...You're with security then. I didn't know. And so young. How clever. Please don't get me wrong. I had no intention of giving away any privileged information. But then, where are my manners?" He reached behind the seat and brought over a silver tray of hard candy. "Have some, won't you?"

I saw this not as a gracious act, but as a way to get me off the subject, so I waved them off. "Then why ask me in the first place?"

"Merely to discuss a basic philosophy of our organization, is all."

"What for?"

"Why, why, for diversion, nothing more. I only asked to see if you knew our mission on how to go about changing Western societies."

"For what reason?"

"To see if you knew, certainly. Think of it as a mental exercise. A way to pass the time, only. A game, if you will."

"And who's to say the information from this 'game,' as you call it, might not get into the wrong hands—like maybe those who attacked our camp. What then?"

"Oh, no, no, you've got me all wrong. I'm talking generalizations, nothing more. We could have discussed such things as the various weaknesses of political systems and how to go about defeating them, that's all I meant. Everyone of any consequence is aware of such things, that is, if their position ranks them near the top of our hierarchy."

"I see." At this point, while he felt the need to backpedal, I'd be foolish not to press him. "While that may sound innocent enough, I feel you're digging for more than that, aren't you? Who are you anyway—other than someone who's good at languages?"

"You must be kidding!" He gasped so, he practically spit on me. "Who am I? Why, I personally assisted in developing the strategies to defeat our Western enemies. My involvement in planning how to alter society throughout Latin American, Europe, and North America has never been questioned. You must be aware of that?"

"Not really."

"Who do you think formulated the vulnerability of Western societies and how to reduce them to anarchy without firing a shot? Me, that's who. And just who do you think ghostwrote the popular series of articles on the steps to dismantle democracies."

Before I could answer, he threw up his hands.

"It's true—others took credit for my contributions. My ideas were stolen by those far less capable. Even my writings were published under pseudonyms. Nevertheless, due to my efforts and mine alone, major progress has been made in degrading governments throughout South and Central America, Europe, and Great Britain. While in other places, namely the United States, where I've been less involved, the process has been slower."

"Yes, yes, but besides that." I pretended impatience. "You haven't explained your odd curiosity that looks, well, to tell the truth, suspicious."

His eyes darted around as if to see who might be listening. "I was very innocently trying to determine your status within the organization, that's all." He lowered his voice. "For the purposes of our having a discussion, nothing more. My motives were completely harmless, I assure you."

"Oh, a discussion?" It occurred to me that this might turn into an opportunity to find out more about what Hect and I had become part of. "About what?"

He adjusted his wire-rim glasses. "Well, for instance, how acquainted you were with our camp system, our policy, and our indoctrination process."

"And that would show what exactly?"

"That you were sufficiently informed to bother entering into an exchange of ideas with, nothing else. Upon my word, I wanted only to describe some basic procedures I developed that I've never received recognition for. Others have, but not me." At this, a look of intensity overcame him. He leaned forward, touching my knee. "For instance, it was my inspiration that after a recruit completes his training, he's to be furnished with authentic-looking documents from prestigious universities, along with degrees, awards, and certificates, etcetera, all of whose authenticity will be impossible to discredit."

I thought of the warehouse in the desert and the boxes of blank certificates.

"Even beyond that," he continued eagerly, "I also developed ingenious methods for slipping qualified graduates across the borders into countries we have targeted for cultural changes. Offices will be completely furnished for them so they can begin their law practices and start the process of instituting our desired reforms."

"Yes, yes, go on, go on." No longer having to pretend interest, I felt the need to restrain my enthusiasm. This was proving easier than I thought. Like most stuffed shirts, with a little prompting, he couldn't shut up about himself. "Such things are very common knowledge, and it'd be hard to prove exactly who had been responsible for them."

He puffed up, and his face reddened. "I've done more, much more, despite the glory due me being usurped by others, especially that fraud Acey Elu. It was my plan to create an attorney army out of unwanted, cast-off youths. I invented the Eliza Doolittle program. Once trained, those recruits would then assimilate into the countries they came from, establish reputable practices, and begin filing approved lawsuits with the intent of permanently changing those societies to meet our ideals."

I wanted to ask who exactly approved them, but that would expose my ignorance.

"No one else but me," he said through clenched teeth. "I alone am responsible for the idea of pitting groups in Western societies against one another by agitating for the rights of oppressed parties. Mine was the lone voice advocating that it would only take a few lawyers to start with, that once the legal profession in general caught wind of a way to line their pockets, they'd eagerly rush to the fray, overrunning the courts. Animosity and hurt feelings among opposing clients would abound. Whichever side won a decision, the loser would seek revenge until the society became hopelessly polarized—race against race, religious against irreligious, conservative versus liberal, male versus female, worker versus management, and on and on the separation goes." He winked. "'A house divided,' as the saying goes."

I hardly had to say a word. The longer he talked the faster his words came as a burning gleam lit up his eyes.

"Me, me! I'm the real mastermind behind the idea of how to make a democracy quiver at the knees, how to send robust economies into decline, how to bait powerful governments into corruption, crushing the populace in despair. A small army of like-minded lawyers will in time gain unstoppable power, becoming judges with lifetime appointments or else politicians who can't be removed from office because of embittered electorates. One day, we'll capture the highest office in the land. You'll see. Now for my most ingenious inspiration of all—this will be accomplished with the respective victim populaces not only unaware, but cheering us on. It was I—I, you hear?—who invented this new modern warfare."

"Well said." I hated to compliment him, but his bragging cleared up a lot of questions in my mind.

"Oh, I could go on," he said excitedly. "There's more, much more, as I've barely scratched the surface. Fortunately, we'll have lots of time to talk as it's a long flight to Bogota."

"Beg pardon?"

"Bogota, Colombia. South America. Our headquarters."

"Oh, yes, of course. Naturally. So that's where we're headed—Bogota." I forced a chuckle. "Now *that* I didn't know."

Final Note

"WORD OF MOUTH" IS HOW this book becomes known. If readers, like you, tell their friends, family and neighbors, then publishers and literary agents will be unable to dictate, at least in the case of this novel, what is to be seen in print. If you choose to help in this, I thank you and consider you a partner in setting authors free to express their heart. Please write to me at whbuzzard@gmail.com and include your email address, plus comments you have about the book. The sequel, *There is a Generation III*, is due out in the spring of 2016.

Reviews at the end of the e-book or at Amazon.com/There is a Generation II are greatly appreciated.

FOR GIFT BOOKS GO TO:
Amazon.com/There is a Generation II

Author Biography

A WILLFUL, UNMANAGEABLE TEENAGER ONCE asked a wise old man how to get control of his unruly habits, his self-destructive behavior, and his inability to complete a task. "Do one thing every day for one hour you don't want to do for someone else," he replied, "and after thirty days, you'll be self-disciplined." Sure enough, it worked.

That teenager grew into the author. WH Buzzard has had a passion ever since to communicate principles as simple and life-changing in fun, readable stories that edify. After all, laughter, like honey, flavors the healing medicine.

A West Texan at heart, the author now lives in Central Texas with his wife, who is one of his most particular editors. When not writing, he'll either be at the pool swimming laps, reading, walking, or attending church

Author biography

Made in USA - Kendallville, IN
72352_9781512180282
01 25 2022 1426